The Hollingsworth Series
Book 4

Michele Linn Griffith

God Is My Rock!

ABOUT THE AUTHOR!

Michele Linn Griffith is a fictional writer, and she's also an avid reader. She lives in Alabama.

mgriffith75@yahoo.com

Philippians 4:13

This story is the product of the authors imagination and all naming of characters, places, incidents and places are all fictitious.

CHAPTER 1

Five years later Sarah, Serena and Ashley are all happily married, and they are still in college. In fact, this is their last year, they all graduate in the end of May, and so they have around couple of months to go and then three or four months later their kids start kindergarten the end of August.

Doug and Elaine's second set of kids are all seniors in high school, they all graduate the first day of June but all of them are hiding a big secret from their parents, siblings, and things are about to get really interesting.

"Hey mom," the kids said. "Oh, hey I didn't hear you all come in," said Elaine.

"Yea we just got in from school,"

they said.

"Okay, so how was your day?" Elaine asked.

"It was fine," they said. "Good," said Elaine.

"Well mom we have a lot of homework, and studying to do, so we're going to our rooms now," they said.

"Okay sure," said Elaine, and the kids started walking away.

As they were walking towards the stairs, Elaine shook her head, okay weird.

CHAPTER 2

On their way to their rooms, Trevor stopped suddenly turning around to look at all his brothers and sister, "whoa, watch out." "What're you doing?" said Trenton.

"Well, I'm actually wondering something," said Trevor.

"Yea, like what?" Trenton said. "Man, we're wondering, what're we going to do?"

"Not sure yet," said Trevor. "Well, me Chelsea, I personally think we need to call our older siblings," said Chelsea.

"Okay, but why though?" Trenton said.

"Well duh, did it ever occur to you that maybe they can help us come up with a solution?" Chelsea asked.

"No Chelsea." "Hello, have you lost your ever-loving mind, if we go to them then they'll immediately go running straight to mom and dad," said Gabe.

"Yea you have a point," said Trevor.

"Yea but Chelsea also has a point too," said Madison.

"Oh wow, you to Madison," said Chelsea.

"Yea, me too," said Madison. "Well, I hate to break it to you, but I feel the same way," said Harper.

"Jeez you to Harper," said Trevor. "Yea, me too," said Harper.

"Okay, who else likes Chelsea's idea?" Trevor asked.

Quickly Trenton and Gabe's hands went up, "oh jeez I can't believe this," said Trevor.

"Okay whatever," and then Trevor stormed off into his room and slammed the door, and then the two quickly followed.

"Okay Chelsea, so how do we go about this?" Madison asked.

"Well, I say we call Sarah, Serena and Ashley, and ask them if we can get together for the weekend and then we go from there," said Chelsea.

"Okay that sounds like a plan," said Harper. "It could work."

"Great, so when do we start?" Madison asked.

"Hello now," said Chelsea.

CHAPTER 3

Thirty minutes later, "alright it looks like we have plans with our older sisters this weekend," Chelsea said.

"Yea, I know, and I can't wait, this

is going to be fun," said Madison.

"Yea we know, we can't wait either."

"Wow, I wish Thursday would hurry up and get here," said Harper.

"Yea, now doubt," said Chelsea. Jut then a knock sounded at the door, "yea who is it?"

"Us, your brothers Trevor, Trenton and Gabe," they said.

"Oh okay, come on in," Chelsea said, and so the door opened up, "Come on in, and shut the door," and so they hurried inside shutting the door quickly, "so what do you want?" Chelsea asked.

"Well, I've thought about your idea and I agree with everything," said Trevor.

"Okay that's good to hear," said

Chelsea.

"Girls were interested in your idea," said Trevor.

The girls smiled, "cool." "So, how do we do this?" asked Trevor.

"Well guys we've already started," said Chelsea.

"Oh really," said Trevor. "Yea you see we called Sarah, Serena and Ashley, and asked to go there this weekend for a girl's weekend," said Chelsea.

"Okay, we see." "So, we need to make plans with K.C, T.J and D.J. this weekend," said Trevor.

"Yes, you guys need to go ahead and call them now," said Chelsea.

"Now?" asked Trevor, Trenton and Gabe.

"Yes now," said Chelsea, Serena

and Sarah.

"Okay then," said the guys, and so Trevor, Trenton and Gabe dialed the numbers of their older brother's.

CHAPTER 4

Thirty minutes later, "alright girls we have plans this weekend with our older brothers, we're having a guy's weekend," said the guys.

"Great," said the girls. "Hey, you guys, we need to go tell mom and dad our plans for this weekend," said Chelsea.

"Okay sure," said the guys, and all six kids walked out of their rooms heading to kitchen.

Minutes later, "hey mom." "Yea kids."

"Mom, we girls have plans this weekend with Sarah, Serena and Ashley, we called and asked if we could come for the weekend and they said yes," said Chelsea.

"Oh okay, well it's fine with me," said Elaine.

"Cool and thanks mom," said the girls.

"Yea sure, you're welcome," said Elaine. "So, what're you boys up to this weekend?"

"Well mom we have plans with D.J., K.C. and T.J., this weekend also," said the guys.

"Oh okay, well that's fine with me too," said Elaine.

"Cool and thanks mom," said the guys.

"Yea sure, you're welcome," said

Elaine. "Wait a minute, did I just hear you right, all six of you are going to be gone this weekend?"

"Yes ma'am, we're leaving Thursday around noontime and we won't be home until late Sunday," said the kids.

"Wow, you mean your dad and I are finally going to get a weekend by ourselves?" Elaine asked.

"Yes ma'am," they said. "Oh wow, that's awesome, thank you kids," said Elaine.

"Yea sure, you're welcome," said the kids.

Elaine was so excited that she dialed Doug's direct line.

A minute or two later, his voice came on the line, "hello this is Detective Hollingsworth speaking."

"Hey honey." "Oh, hey babe, what's up?" he asked.

"Nothing much, but I do have a wonderful surprise for you," said Elaine.

"Oh yea." "So, what's this wonderful surprise of yours?" asked Doug.

"Well, get this, all six kids will be gone this whole weekend," said Elaine.

"Oh wow." "So, you know what this means?" Doug asked. "Yea this means we get the whole weekend by ourselves," said Elaine.

"Yes, and it sounds wonderful," said Doug. "Wait a minute your serious."

"Yea," said Elaine. "Really?" Doug asked. "Seriously we actually get a whole weekend by ourselves?"

"Yes honey," said Elaine. "Great," said Doug. "Well then I'm taking off this Thursday through the weekend."

"Oh okay, why though?" Elaine asked.

"Well, you and I are going out of town for a much-needed vacation," said Doug.

"Oh wow." "Oh my, gosh, thank you so much, that sounds wonderful," said Elaine.

"Yea, I know," said Doug. "Well babe, I'll see you in a little while."

"Okay great," said Elaine, and then she hung up.

"Hey kids." "Yes ma'am," they said. "Kids I'm letting you know that your dad and I are leaving early Thursday morning for a much-needed vacation," Elaine.

"Okay cool," said the kids,

CHAPTER 5

The next three days went by quick and before they knew it Thursday March eighth was upon them, and Elaine and Doug were up getting ready for their much-needed trip.

"Doug." "Yea babe," said Doug. "Doug, I can't help wondering, what the kids are up too?" Elaine said.

"What do you mean?" Doug asked.

"Well, they never asked to go spend time with their older siblings unless they have problems or issues, so that's what's making me think that their up to something or their hiding something but I'm not sure what it is yet," said Elaine.

"Yea now that you mention it, you're right, I believe they're hiding something but for right now we're not going to worry about it, instead we're going to enjoy our long weekend vacation alone," said Doug.

"Yea, no doubt and I can't wait," said Elaine.

"Alright then let's get ready to go then," said Doug.

"Yea sure, but I'm ready," said Elaine.

"Yea, me too," said Doug.

CHAPTER 6

Fifteen minutes later Elaine and Doug were leaving the driveway, "good they're gone."

"As soon as we get out at noon we're heading straight to our sisters, and brother's homes, so go ahead and load the cars now," said Chelsea.

"Yea, we agree," said the group. "Good," said Chelsea.

CHAPTER 7

Twenty minutes later all six kids were heading out to school.

CHAPTER 8

Elaine and Doug were little under halfway to their location, "honey."

"Yea dear," said Doug. "Honey, I'm wondering, where are we going anyway?" Elaine asked.

"It's a surprise, we'll be there around twelve or so," said Doug.

"Oh, okay great, I can't wait," said Elaine.

"Yea, me either," said Doug.

CHAPTER 9

Twelve o'clock rolled around and the kids were walking out the school doors, "yes we're finally heading out to Carson City, which is an honor drive," said Ashley.

"Yes, we know this Ashley," said Gabe.

"Okay, well see you guys there," said the girls.

"Okay bye," said the guys.

CHAPTER 10

"Honey we're finally here," said Doug.

"Okay, where are we exactly?" Elaine asked.

"Blue Laguna Island," said Doug. Elaine smiled, "wow this is amazing."

"Yea, it is, so let's go enjoy ourselves," said Doug.

Elaine smiled, "yea that sounds great."

"Good," he said.

CHAPTER 11

It was a little after one when the two vehicles arrived in Carson City.

Chelsea quickly dialed five on her car phone.

Within minutes her brother Trevor's voice came through the line answering, "hello."

"Hey sis," he said. "So, what can I do for you?"

"Well, I was just letting you know that we're not from Sarah, Serena and Ashley's place of stay," said Chelsea.

"Oh wow," said Trevor. "Yea they live in the neighborhood of Cascade Landings, which they live in the first connecting houses on the right," said Chelsea.

"Okay great," said Trevor. "Well now T.J, K.C. and D.J. live across town in the neighborhood of Casper Inn, and they live in the last connecting houses on the left."

"Okay, well that's cool," said Chelsea.

"Yea, it is," said Trevor. "Well anyway, we're on our way."

"Okay be careful," said Chelsea.
"Yea, you too," said Trevor.

CHAPTER 12

"Hey girls, we'll be there in a little bit, are you two ready to go?" said Chelsea.

"Yea, we are," said Madison and Harper.

"Great," me too," said Chelsea.

CHAPTER 13

Ten minutes later the little red Honda pulled through the iron gates, "oh my, gosh, girls we're finally here," said Chelsea.

"Yay cool," said Madison and Harper, and so Chelsea quickly parked int the huge driveway.

Minutes later they were getting out of their car, suddenly the house door opened up, and there stood three smiling faces.

A couple of minutes later the three young girls started walking up.

Within several strides they walked up, "hey girls," said Chelsea, Madison and Harper.

"Hey yourselves, it's so good to see you girls made here for a visit," said Ashley, Serena and Sarah.

"Yea, us too," said Chelsea, Madison and Harper, and then quickly hugs were passed around. Afterwards they pulled apart, "well come on in let's get you girls settled," said Ashley.

"Yes, that would be good," said Chelsea, Madison and Harper.

"Girls, in a little while we are going to get together," said Ashley.

"Okay sure, that sounds good," said Chelsea, Madison and Harper.

Ashley smiled, "good."

CHAPTER 14

"Hey guys, we're here," said Trevor.

"Great," said Trenton and Gabe. "Well let's go in," said Trevor, and so Trevor turned into the Casper Inn driveway and drove through the iron gates.

A few minutes later black suv pulled into the huge parking space.

Minutes later they were getting out of their car, when suddenly the door opened up, and three tall figures walked out, and so the three young guys headed up the walkway.

A few long strides later they were stepping on the top step, "hey guys," said Trevor, Trenton and Gabe.

"Hey yourselves, it's good to see you three, we're glad you came to see us this weekend," said T.J., K.C. and D.J.

"Yea, us too," said Trevor, Trenton and Gabe, and then hugs were quickly passed around.

Afterwards they pulled away, "well come on in let's get you three guys settled," said K.C., T.J. and D.J.

"Yea that sounds good," said Trevor, Trenton and Gabe.

K.C., T.J., and D.J. smiled, "great."

CHAPTER 15

The six girls were all sitting outside enjoying the pool, cooking out and watching their young nieces and nephews playing, when Sarah cleared her throat, "now girls please tell us your real reason for your sudden visit," said Ashley.

"What do you ever mean?" asked Chelsea.

"Well, we know you three are hiding something but we're not sure what exactly," said Ashley.

"Well, what makes you think that?" asked Chelsea.

"Well girls for starters you girls don't usually come to visit unless you're in trouble of some kind," said Ashley.

"Oh okay, you're right, we're hiding a huge secret," said Chelsea.

"Uh huh, we knew it," said Ashley. "So, spill it, what's going on?"

"I'll be the spokesperson for us, so here it goes," Chelsea said, and so she took a couple of deep calming breaths and then said, "alright you see us girls and our brothers are hiding a huge secret."

"Oh jeez," said Ashley, Serena and Sarah. "Anyway Chelsea, you need to start from the beginning."

"Okay, here it goes, you see last year the beginning of our senior year, we girls and our brothers met up with some people, which they're associated with a bad group and we're dating them," said Chelsea.

"Oh wow." "Okay, let us get this

straight, you girls and your bothers got yourselves mixed up with a bad group of people and now you're dating them behind mom and dad's backs, right?" said Ashley.

"Yes, that about sums it up but there's more to the story," said Chelsea.

"Oh great," said Ashley. "Well go ahead and spill it."

"Well, we kinda got into drugs and we're kinda sexually active," said Chelsea.

"Oh jeez, this isn't happening," said Ashley. "Really?" "Seriously?" "Are you kidding us?"

"No, we're afraid not, we wish we were though," said Chelsea.

"Excuse us," said Ashley. "What were you thinking?"

"Duh, we weren't," said Chelsea.
"Yea, you're right, you weren't," said
Ashley.

"We made a mistake, granite a
big one," said Chelsea.

"Oh yea, we should say so," said
Ashley. "You girls do realize that
you're going to have to tell mom and
dad sooner or later."

"Yea, we know but we just
thought we could come talk to you
first," said Chelsea.

"Yea you girls did the right thing,"
said Ashley.

"Thanks," said Chelsea, Madison
and Harper.

"Yea sure," said Ashley, Serena
and Sarah. "Alright listen here's what
we're going to do, you girls are going
to give the names of your new guys

and the new girls, and we're going to setup doctor appointments for today."

"Okay sure, but why though?" asked Chelsea, Harper and Madison.

"Well first to make sure we don't have anymore surprises in the works and to fin out who these new people are that you kids are actually dating," said Ashley.

"Okay great but to be honest we've only been with one guy and that's our boyfriends," said Chelsea.

"Okay, well that's good to hear but there's still the chance that you could get into trouble and finding yourselves in a serious situation," said Ashley.

"Oh okay, whatever," said Chelsea.

"Anyway, here we go, Sarah your

job is to call the OB-GYN Clinic and make three appointments for today," said Ashley.

"Sure, no problem, I'll start now," said Sarah.

"Okay great," said Ashley. "Now you girls need to give me the list of those guys and girls that you've gotten mixed up with."   "Yea sure, we'll start on them now," said Chelsea.

"Girls just so you know we're really glad you all came to us first," said Ashley.

"Thanks, us too," said Chelsea. "Good we're going to do our best to help you through this crazy disturbing mess," said Ashley.

"Okay, that sounds good to us," said Chelsea. "And f.y.i. our brothers are over at T.J., K.C. and D.J.'s place of stay talking to them also."

"Oh wow, that's great," said Ashley. "Well maybe we can work together."

"Yea maybe," said Serena. "Yea really," said Sarah. "Girls for the time being we don't say anything to mom and dad about any of this until we have all the facts and information," said Ashley.

"Okay, yea no doubt that sounds good to us," said Chelsea. "Great," said Ashley, suddenly Sarah walked back outside to the rest of the group, "okay you girls have doctor appointments at three o'clock with Doctor Jonah Anderson, he's who we use," said Sarah.

"Okay great and thanks," said Chelsea.

"Yea sure, you're welcome anytime," said Sarah.

"Ashley here's the list you wanted, I wrote down both our boyfriends and our brothers names also," said Chelsea.

"Oh good, and thanks," Ashley said. "Alright well let's see we have Dante Eastland, Derek Crowder, Aaron Garrison, Erin Deaton, Jana Peterson and Deanne Camps."

"Thanks for your corporation." "Yea sure," said Chelsea. "Now while I'm doing this huge search, Serena and Sarah will go with you to your doctor's appointments," said Ashley.

"Great and thanks," said Chelsea. "Yea sure, no problem," said Sarah. "Girls, we leave in an hour."

"Okay," said Chelsea.

CHAPTER 16

Ashley was sitting at her computer, shaking her head, "Chelsea, Madison and Harper it seems that you girls so far have managed to pick real winners," said Ashley.

"Oh yea," said Chelsea, Madison and Harper.

"Yea these punks and punkettes have rap sheets miles and miles long, but so far it looks like just petty minor stupid stuff but still not good," said Ashley. "Jeez," all the while shaking her head in disbelief.

"Yea, we know but we can't help who our hearts love," said Chelsea.

"True," said Ashley. Suddenly Sarah's phone started ringing, and so she pulled her phone out and answered, "hello."

"Hey Sarah, it's T.J.," he said. "Oh, hey," said Sarah. "So, what's up?" "How's it going?"

"Nothing much, and everything was going good until the guys got here," said T.J.

"Yea, I know the feeling, the girls are here with us," said Sarah.

"Oh great," said T.J. "Yea, you can say that again," said Sarah.

"Well anyway, it seems that we have a crazy disturbing situation on our hands and all due to our younger brothers and sisters."

"Yea, I know," said T.J. "So, how do we want to handle this?"

"I'm not sure yet but we have started working on somethings," said Sarah.

"Oh really, like what exactly?" T.J. asked.

"Well, we've started doing research on these punks and punkettes that they've gotten themselves mixed up with and we've also setup the girls doctor appointments for today," said Sarah.

"Great, that's good to know," said T.J. "Well anyway, the boys have been up front telling us everything and they're ninety five percent sure they got those three girls pregnant."

"Oh jeez, this isn't happening," said Sarah.   "Yea, well I'm afraid it is," said T.J.

"Oh jeez, this isn't good," said Sarah.

"Yea, no duh, yuh think," said T.J. "Sarah, is it possible for us to come over there and sit down and talk and work on this horrible situation together?"

"Yea sure," said Sarah. "Great, see you girls soon," said T.J.

"Okay, see you guys soon," said Sarah, and then she hung up.

"Who was that?" asked Ashley. T.J., and he and the rest of the boy group is coming over to hopefully to help is come up with some kinda solution to this crazy disturbing mess of you girls."

"Oh wow." "Okay, well that sounds good," said Ashley.

"Hey girls, not to interrupt but it's to leave for your doctor appointments," said Ashley.

"Okay, we're ready," said Chelsea, Madison and Harper.

"Great," said Ashley. "Serena and Sarah, if and when you find out anything, please let me know."

"Sure, of course, bye," said Sarah.

CHAPTER 17

As the five girls were leaving out, as Ashley's phone started ringing, and so she answered, "hello."

"Hey dear," said Elaine. "Oh, hey mom, what's up?" said Ashley.

"Nothing much, we're just checking in on you girls," said Elaine. "Oh okay, well everyone's fine here," said Ashley.

"Good, that's good to hear," Elaine said.

"Well, anyone mom everyone's gone but me and I'm babysitting and working on schoolwork," said Ashley.

"Oh okay," said Elaine. "So, mom how's your trip?" asked Ashley.

"Oh wow, it's amazing, we couldn't have asked for better," said Elaine.

"Well good, I'm glad to hear, and we're so glad you two got to finally have husband and wife time," Ashley said.

"Yea, me too," said Elaine. "Great," said Ashley. "Well mom, I hate to cut this short, but I really have to get back to my schoolwork and attending to kids."

"Oh sure, no problem, we'll check in later," said Elaine. "Okay, well anyway love you, have fun."

"Okay, and yea you too, bye," said Ashley.

CHAPTER 18

When Elaine got off the phone, she looked over at Doug, "well everything and everyone seems to be fine but I'm definitely certain that somethings going on with that bunch but I'm not quite sure what exactly," said Elaine.

"Well babe, there probably is something going on but we're not going to worry about them or anything else until after our trip," said Doug.

"Okay, yea sure," said Elaine.

CHAPTER 19

A knock sounded at the door, and so Ashley hurried over and quickly opened it up and there stood the six guys, "hey guys."

"Hey sis," said T.J. "Well good to see you guys," said Ashley.

"Thanks," he said. "The other girls aren't back yet," said Ashley.

"Alright, no problem," said T.J. Suddenly Ashley's phone started ringing, and so she pulled out her phone and answered," "hello."

"Hey Ashley, it's Sarah, and I'm calling to let you know we're on our way home," said Sarah.

"Oh good." "So, what did you find out?" asked Ashley.

"A lot and none of it good," said Sarah.

"Oh great," said Ashley. "Alright, see you soon," said Sarah.

"Yea, see you soon," said Ashley,

and then she hung up.

"Who was that Ashley?" asked T.J. "Guys that was Sarah," said Ashley.

"Oh good," said T.J. "So, what did they find out?"

"Well, she said they found out a lot and none of it good," said Ashley.

"Oh great," said T.J. "Yea really," said Ashley. "Well, they'll be here soon."

"Okay good," said T.J.

CHAPTER 20

Thirty minutes later Ashley and the other four walked through the door Chelsea, Harper and Madison all had a tear-streaked faces, "girls, what's wrong?" asked Ashley.

"Well, we just found out some real horrible news," said Chelsea, Harper and Madison.

"Oh yea, what kinda horrible news are we talking about?" asked Ashley.

"Well, it seems that we are all are around three months pregnant," said Chelsea, Harper and Madison.

"Oh wow." "Oh no, we're sorry to hear about that," said Ashley.

"Thanks, and yea us too," said Chelsea, Harper and Madison. "Man, we're really scared, and we really don't know what we're going to do."

"Oh girls, don't worry we'll figure out something, we promise," said Ashley, Serena and Sarah.

"Yea okay, we hope so," said Chelsea, Harper and Madison.

"We will, don't worry," said Ashley, Serena and Sarah.

"Okay, yea that's easy for you to say, man we really messed up," said Chelsea, Harper and Madison.

"Yea we should say so," said Ashley, Serena and Sarah.

"Oh my, gosh, what're we going to tell mom and dad?"

"Most importantly, how're we going to tell them?" said Chelsea, Madison and Harper.

"Yea not sure yet but we'll come up with something," said Sarah, Ashley and Serena.

"Ah, Serena, Sarah and Ashley, we've only got two and a half days to figure this mess out," said Chelsea.

"Oh wow." "Great, this is just great," said Ashley. Suddenly Trevor's phone started ringing, and so he pulled out his phone and answered, "hello."

"Hey Trevor, It's Jana," she said. "Oh, hey babe, what's up?" said Trevor.

"Nothing much," said Jana. "Anyway, listen up, the reason I'm calling is to let you know that I'm around three months pregnant."

"Oh wow." "Jeez," said Trevor. "Yea, we need to get together soon and talk," said Jana.

"Yea we do, I'll be home Sunday afternoon," said Trevor.

"Okay great, see you then," said Jana, and then she hung up.

"Who was that Trevor?" asked T.J. "My girlfriend Jana, and she was calling to let me know that she's around three months pregnant," said Trevor.

"Oh wow, that's some scary news," said T.J.

"Yea tell me about it," said Trevor, but before anything else could be said, Trenton's phone started ringing, and so he answered, "hello."

"Hey Trenton, it's Deanne," she said.

"Oh, hey babe, what's up?" he said.

"Nothing much but I do have something to tell you," Deanne said.

"Oh yea, like what?" Trenton asked.

"Well, I just found out I'm around three months pregnant," said Deanne.

"Oh jeez," said Trenton. "Yea jeez is right," said Deanne. "Listen we need to talk soon."

"Alright, well we'll be home Sunday afternoon," Trenton said.

"Okay great, see you then," said Deanne.

"Yea sure," said Trenton, and then he hung up.

"Who was that Trenton?" asked T.J.

"Well, that was my girlfriend Deanne calling to tell me that she's around three months pregnant and that we need to get together and talk soon," said Trenton.

"Oh wow, that's crazy," said T.J. "Yea, no duh, yuh think," said Trenton, but before anything else could be said, Gabe's phone started ringing, and so he answered, "hello."

"Hey Gabe, it's Erin," she said.

"Oh, hey babe, what's up?" said Gabe.

"Nothing really but I do have to tell you something hard," said Erin.

"Oh okay, like what?" asked Gabe. "Well Gabe, I just found out that I'm around three months pregnant," said Erin.

"Oh great," said Gabe. "Yea really," said Erin. "Anyway, we really need to get together and talk soon."

"Sure alright, I'll be home Sunday afternoon," said Gabe.

"Okay great, see you then," said Erin.

"Yea, see you then," said Gabe, and then he hung up. "Gabe, who was that?" T.J. asked.

"Well, that was my girlfriend Erin calling to let me know that she's around three months pregnant and that we need to get together and talk soon," said Gabe.

"Okay great." "Wow man, this is a dossier of a mess," said T.J.

"Yea you can say that again," said Gabe.

"Man, we three don't know what we're going to do about his huge mess up, but we'll figure something out," said Trevor.

"Okay good for you guys," said T.J., K.C. and D.J.

"Thanks," said Trevor, Trenton and Gabe.

"Yea sure, you're welcome," said T.J., K.C. and D.J.

CHAPTER 21

"Girls Chelsea, Madison and Harper we guys think you girls should call these so-called idiot boyfriends of yours and let them know about your pregnancies," said Trevor, Trenton and Gabe.

"Ah girls, they're right you three girls need to make calls to those guys," said Ashley, Sarah and Serena.

"Oh okay, sure here goes nothing," said Chelsea, and so she dialed her boyfriend Derek's number.

Within minutes his voice came through the line, "hello."

"Hey Derek, it's Chelsea." "Oh, hey babe, what's up?" he asked.

"Nothing much," she said. "Listen I have something to tell you, and it's something really scary and hard."

"Okay sure, what is it?" he asked.

"Well Derek I'm around three months pregnant," said Chelsea.

"Oh wow." "Jeez, this is a surprise," he said.

"Yea, I know," said Chelsea. "Anyway, we need to talk as soon as possible."

"Alright, when?" he asked. "Soon," she said.

"Alright, so where are you right now?" he asked.

"I'm in Carson City with my older sisters," said Chelsea. "Okay."

"Well, I can be there in an hour just text me the address," he said.

"Okay sure, see you soon," Chelsea said.

"Yea sure babe, see you soon," he said, and then she hung up, and then turned around and looked at everyone, "wow that was easy but the hardest thing I've had to do," Chelsea said.

"Yea, we bet," said the group. "So, what did he have to say?"

"Well, he's shocked but he's on his way here now to talk," said Chelsea.

"Okay great," said the group. "Yea, I guess," said Chelsea.

"Alright Madison, you're turn." "Okay, well here goes nothing," said Madison, and so she dialed Aaron's number.

Within minutes his voice came through line, "hello."

"Hey Aaron, it's Madison." "Oh, hey babe, what's up?" he asked.

"Nothing much but there's something I have to tell you and it's scary and hard," said Madison.

"Alright shoot," he said. "Okay, well here it goes I just found out I'm around three months pregnant," said Chelsea. "Really?" "Seriously?"

"Are you kidding me?" he asked. "No joke," she said. "I'm serious." "Look we need to talk soon."

"Alright sure, when?" asked Aaron. "Soon," she said,

"Okay, where are you Madison?" he asked.

"I'm in Carson City with my older sisters," said Madison.

"Oh okay, well I'll come there today just text me the address," he said.

"Okay, yea sure, see you soon," said Madison, and then she hung up and then turned around to everyone, "wow that was the hardest and scariest call I've had to make," said Madison.

"Okay great," said the group. "So, what did he have to say?"

"Well, he was shocked but he's on his way here to talk," Madison said,

"Great," they said. "Yea, I guess," said Madison. "Okay Harper, you're turn."

"Okay, sure well here goes nothing," said Harper, and so she dialed Dante's number.

Within minutes his voice came through the line, "Hello."

"Hey Dante, it's Harper." "Oh, hey babe, what's up?" he asked.

"Oh, nothing much," she said. "Listen, I have something really scary and hard to tell you."

"Okay, sure what?" asked Dante. "Well Dante, I just found out I'm around three months pregnant," said Harper.

"Oh wow." "Oh my, gosh, I'm not believing this," he said. "This can't be happening."

"Yea, well I'm afraid it is," said Harper. "Dante, we need to talk soon."

"Okay, when?" he asked. "Well, right now I'm at my older sisters house in Carson City and I'll be back Sunday afternoon," said Harper.

"Okay, well that's too long to wait, so why don't I come there today, so just text me the address," he said.

"Okay sure, see you soon," said Harper, and then she hung up, and then turned around to her siblings, "wow that was a crazy call and probably the hardest and scariest call I've had to do."

"Okay great, and yea we bet," they said. "So, what did he have to say?"

"Well, he's totally shocked but he agreed that we need to talk, and so he's on his way here," said Harper.

"Okay great," said Ashley, Serena and Sarah.

"Now listen Trenton, Trevor and Gabe, we're going to foreworn you now, now that since the girls boyfriends are on their way, we wouldn't be surprised if your girlfriends decide to come today also."

"Yea, we agree," said T.J., K.C. and D.J.

"Okay thanks, but we're seeing

them this Sunday afternoon," said Trevor, Trenton and Gabe.

"Alright but we think they'll come today with the three guys," said Ashley, Serena and Sarah.

"Sure okay, whatever you say but we don't think so," said Trevor, Trenton and Gabe.

"Alright, well we'll see," said Ashley, Serena and Sarah.

"Yea, we will," said Trevor, Trenton and Gabe.

"Okay, well now that chore's done, and while we're waiting for our guests to arrive, why don't we chat for a while?" said Ashley, Serena and Sarah.

"Sure, what about?" said Chelsea, Madison and Harper.

"Well girls, we want to know,

when is your due dates?" asked Ashley.

"Um, around May or June, but we'll know more closer to time," said Chelsea, Madison and Harper.

"Okay great," said Ashley, Serena and Sarah.

Ashley, Serena and Sarah smiled, "great." "Now, we have questions for you older siblings."

"Okay, what?" asked Ashley, Serena and Sarah.

"Well, do you three have any ideas on how to tell mom and dad about this crazy situation?" asked Chelsea, Madison and Harper.

"No, we're not sure yet, but we're still working on that one," said Ashley.

"Oh my, gosh." "Wow it just hit me, do you realize that in just under two hours or so your so-called boyfriends and maybe girlfriends will be here."

"Yea, we know," said Chelsea, Madison, Harper, Trevor, Trenton and Gabe.

"Good, well then we suggest we do this huge meeting out here in the backyard," said Ashley.

"Okay sure, that sounds good," said Chelsea, Madison, Harper, Trenton, Trevor and Gabe.

"Great," said Ashley.

CHAPTER 22

"Everyone I'm watching for our guests," said Chelsea.

"Okay Chelsea let us know when they get here," said Ashley.

"Sure," said Chelsea.

CHAPTER 23

Around six fifteen, a black van pulled into the huge driveway, "hey everyone they're here," said Chelsea. "Alright great," said the group.

A minute or two later six people exited the van and quickly started walking towards the door, "oh my, gosh, this is great," said Chelsea.

"What Chelsea?" asked Trevor. "Well let's just say the guys are in for a surprise," said Chelsea.

"Oh yea, how?" Trevor asked. "You'll see," said Chelsea, and so Trevor hurried over to the window, "Chelsea what're talking about?"

"Come see," she replied, and so

he looked out the window, "oh jeez, I'm not believing this," he said. Suddenly they heard, what?" came from Trenton and Gabe.

"Well let's just say the girls were right," said Trevor.

"Oh no." "Wait, are you serious?" asked Trenton and Gabe.

"Yea, no duh, that's funny, we told you so," said Chelsea.

"Yea whatever," said Trevor, Trenton and Gabe.

"Yea but we did," said Chelsea. "Okay so," said Trevor. "Chelsea smiled. Suddenly a knock sounded at the door, and so Chelsea quickly hurried over to the door and opened it up, "hey everyone, and good afternoon, thanks for coming," said Chelsea.

"Yea sure, thanks for having us," said Dante, Derek and Aaron.

"Well welcome, come in," Chelsea said.

"Thanks," said the group, and then they walked through the door.

"Well now, everyone please meet our boyfriends Derek, Dante and Aaron," said Chelsea, Sarah and Serena.

"You three guys, please meet our older siblings Ashley, Serena, Sarah, K.C., T.J. and D.J.

"Well, it's really nice to meet you three guys," said the group.

"Yea, thanks and you too," said the guys.

"Well now, we're next," said Trevor, Trenton and Gabe.

"Alright, we're ready," said the

group.

"Good, well everyone please meet our girlfriends Jana, Deanne and Eric," said Trevor, Trenton and Gabe, "You three girls, please meet our older siblings T.J., K.C., D.J., Serena, Sarah and Ashley."

"Well, it's really nice to meet you girls," said the group.

"Yea, thank and you too," said the girls.

"Well now, come on let's go out to the backyard," said Ashley. "Alright," said the group.

Once everyone was seated, "everyone I know this is a big shock to all of you because it was too us, but we need to work together and find a solution to this crazy disturbing mess that you all have managed to get yourselves into," said Ashley.

"Yes, we know, please don't remind us, this is why we're here," said the younger sibling group.

"Good," said Ashley. "Now girls and guys we suggest you all work together as a team."

"Okay, and yea we plan on it," said the younger sibling group.

"Great," said the older sibling group.

"Excuse me, can I speak, I have something to say," said Derek.

"Sure, go on," said Ashley. "Okay thanks," said Derek.

"Well now, I'm speaking for Dante, Aaron and myself, so first off I know we're not the kind of guys you would have or want for your younger sisters, but I assure you they'll be taken care of along with these babies, we love them, and we want these babies, we'll step up and help out with any and everything."

"Oh wow, that's awesome, that's what we were hoping for, and thank you so much," said Ashley, Serena and Sarah.

"Yea sure, no problem, but the way I see it we owe you a big thank you," said Derek.

"Yea sure, you're welcome but we wouldn't have it any other way," said Ashley, Serena and Sarah.

"Excuse me, I have something to say," said Trevor.

"Alright, go on," said T.J. "Okay, well I'm speaking for Gabe, Trenton and myself, and anyway, first off we love you girls Jana, Erin and Deanne, we want these babies and we're going to step up and help out with any and everything."

"Oh wow, we are so proud of you guys, you're growing up right before our eyes," said the older siblings group.

"Thank you this is what we were hoping for," said Trevor, Trenton and Gabe.

"Great," said the older siblings group. Suddenly, they heard, "excuse us, we have something to ask our ladies," said Trevor, Trenton and Gabe.

"Okay sure, go ahead," said the older sibling group.

"Alright, well Chelsea, Madison and Harper, you know we love you ladies dearly," said Derek, Dante and

Aaron.

"Yes, and we love you guys too," said Chelsea, Madison and Harper.

Derek, Dante and Aaron smiled, "great."

"Well ladies, we need to know, will you do us the honor of becoming our wives?"

Suddenly tears started streaming down their faces and, "yes," came from their lips, and then the three ladies ran and launched themselves into their boyfriends arms hugging, and kissing them, when suddenly cheers, whistles, clapping and congratulations came from around the room for the newly engaged couples.

"Thanks," came from the new couples.

Suddenly they heard, "alright

excuse us, we're next," said Trevor, Trenton and Gabe.

"Yea sure, go on," said T.J., K.C. and D.J.

"Alright, well here goes nothing, Jana, Eric and Deanne, you ladies know we love you dearly," said Trevor, Trenton and Gabe.

"Yes, and we love you guys too," said Jana, Deanne and Erin. Trevor, Trenton and Gabe smiled, "great." "So, ladies, what do you say, will you marry us and make us the happiest guys on the face of the earth?"

Suddenly tears started streaming down their faces, and immediately, "yes," came from the ladies, and then they immediately ran over and launched themselves into their boyfriend's arms hugging and kissing them, and then suddenly clapping, cheers, whistles and congratulations came from all around for the newly engaged couples. "Thanks," said the new couples.

"Well congratulations is in order for all of you, welcome to our family Erin, Jana, Deanne, Derek, Dante and Aaron," said Ashley, Serena, Sarah, T.J., K.C. and D.J.

"Thanks," they said. "Man, this has been a very interesting day with so much happening," said Ashley.

"Ah, yea I should say so," said T.J. "Oh wow."

"Oh jeez, you guys do realize that Chelsea, Madison, Harper, Trenton, Gabe and Trevor are all engaged and expecting babes between May and June and to top it off mom and dad have no clue about any of this," said Ashley.

"Oh jeez, you're right this has been something of an unusual day," said T.J.

"Ah, yea you can say that again," said Ashley.

"So, by the way, how are we going to break the news of this crazy disturbing mess of a situation to mom and dad?" asked T.J.

"Not sure yet," said Ashley. "Well, you all better be figuring out something, they're going to be home Sunday," said T.J.

"Oh jeez, you're right," said Ashley. "Yea duh," said T.J.

CHAPTER 24

"It's around ten thirty and the group of six were leaving for the night, "well guys and girls it was really nice meeting you, have a safe trip home," said the older siblings.

"Yea, you too, bye," said the girls and guys, and then they walked out the door.

After closing the door, Ashley turned around, "wow this has been one crazy disturbing interesting day."

"Yea you can say that again," said the younger siblings.

"Wow we can't believe you six are all engaged and expecting babies," said Ashley.

"Yea, us too," said the younger siblings. Suddenly the phone started ringing, and so she pulled out her phone and answered it, "hello."

"Hey Ashley, it's mom." "Oh, hey mom," she said.

"So, how's everything going?" asked Elaine.

"Fine," said Ashley. "Good," said Elaine.

"So, mom, how's yours and dads trips?" asked Ashley.

"Wonderful," said Elaine. "Great," said Ashley.

"Listen dear, we've decided to stay another couple of days," said Elaine.

"Oh wow, that's great," said Ashley.

"Yea, we think so," said Elaine. "Okay, so when will you be home?" asked Ashley.

"Thursday or Friday," said Elaine. "Why do you ask dear?"

"Oh no reason, just curious is all," said Ashley.

"Alrighty then," said Elaine. "Well, we'll be checking in periodically."

"Great." "Well, have fun," said Ashley.

"Thanks, we will, and you too dear," said Elaine. "Well dear, I'm going to get off here for now, talk to you soon."

"Yea sure," said Ashley, and then they hung up. "Who was that Ash?" asked Trevor.

"That was mom and dad," Ashley said.

"Great." "So, what did they have to say?" asked Trevor.

"Nothing much, they were just checking in on us and letting us know that they're staying a couple of days longer," said Ashley.

"Great, that's great to hear," said Trevor. "So, when will they be home exactly?"

"Well, my understanding is they'll be home Thursday or Friday," said Ashley.

"Great." "Well then that means we have more time," said Trevor.

"Yea, we do," said Ashley. "Anyway, I have an idea on how you need to tell mom and dad about your crazy situation."

"Okay, Ashley let's hear it," said Trevor.

"Sure." "Well, I think you six need to write a letter to mom and dad explaining everything from the beginning to ending leaving nothing out," said Ashley.

"Alright that sounds like a good idea," said Trevor. "In fact, actually it's a wonderful idea."

"Okay great," said Ashley. "Letter writing," said Gabe.

"Yes Gabe, letter writing," said Trevor. "Man, it's like telling our side of the story only in letter form."

"Alright," we see," said the group. "Good then, so why don't you six go get started on them now?" said Ashley.

"Okay, yea you're right we don't have much longer until they come home, so let's start on them today," said Chelsea.

"Yea sure, whatever," said Trenton and Gabe.

CHAPTER 25

Sunday afternoon rolled around, the group of six walked into the family room each holding a notebook, "hey Ashley."

"Yea," Ashley said. "Uh here's our letter things for mom and dad," said the six.

"Oh good, and thanks," said Ashley. "Yea sure," they said. "Say Ashley, would you mind looking over them for us?"

"No, I wouldn't mind." "In fact, I would love too," said Ashley.

"Thanks," said the group. "Yea sure, you're welcome, no problem," Ashley said, and for the rest of the afternoon and evening the siblings took advantage of the pool and enjoyed spending time with one another and their siblings.

CHAPTER 26

March eleventh, Monday morning rolled around, "hey girls."

"Yea Ashley," said Chelsea. Madison and Harper.

"You girls need to start getting all of your stuff together for when you go homed and that means cleaning the rooms and bathrooms," said Ashley.

"Alrighty," said Chelsea, Madison and Harper.

"Great," said Ashley. "Oh, before we forget our boyfriends asked if they could come over soon."

"Yea that's fine," said Ashley. "Great because we kinda already told them that they could come over," said Chelsea, Madison and Harper.

"Okay, well then girls go ahead and let your brothers know that they can invite their girlfriends over too," said Ashley.

"Okay sure," said Chelsea, Madison and Harper.

"Well now since we're going to have company here shorty, so we need to get a move on cleaning up," Ashley said.

"Yea sure," said the girls. "Hey Ashley."

"Yea girls," said Ashley. "Uh we need you to call the school and let them know that we're going to be out the rest of the week," they said.

"Yea sure, nor problem, I'll handle it now," said Ashley.

"Great and thanks," the girls said. "Yea, you're welcome," said Ashley.

As the girls were walking away, suddenly they heard, "oh, wait a minute girls," and they immediately turned around, "yea,"

"Girls, I forgot to mention a couple of things," said Ashley.

"Sure, what?" asked Chelsea. "Well first I forgot to tell you your letters were great and straight to the point, you took our suggestions well, and secondly you girls have doctor appointments tomorrow morning at nine o'clock," said Ashley.

"Oh okay, great and thanks," said Chelsea, Madison and Harper, and then they turned around and started walking away.

CHAPTER 27

Before they knew it lunchtime was upon them, "jeez it's lunchroom and our guest will be here anytime," said Ashley.

"Yea, we know," said the six. "Well, we need to get cleaned up and changed," said Chelsea.

"Yea, so what're we waiting for let's go do that then," said Trevor said.

CHAPTER 28

Thirty minutes later the doorbell rang and shortly after Chris opened the door to the group of six loaded down with bags, "welcome, come on in," said Chris.

"Sure, and thanks for having us," they said.

"Yea sure, you must be the kids,

I've heard so much about," said Chris.

"Yea, we guess so," said the group. "Good." "Well now, I'm Chris Sarah's husband, and this is Chase Serena's husband and Damien here belongs to Ashley."

"Hi, I'm Dante, this is Derek, Aaron, Erin, Deanne and Jana, and we're here to see Chelsea, Madison, Harper, Trevor, Trenton and Gabe.

"Well now, it's really nice to finally meet you kids," said Chris.

"Yes sir, you too, and we hope you don't mind we just wanted to come and spend the day with you all," said Dante.

"Oh no, it's no problem, we're glad to have you all," said Chris.

"Thanks," said the group. Just then, "ahem," came from behind the three men, and so they turned around, "oh hey babes, our guests are here," said Chris. "Great," said Serena, Sarah and Ashley.

"Wow this is amazing." "This is really nice with the connecting doors, it makes it look like one huge house," said the group.

"Thanks," said Serena, Sarah and Ashley.

"We like it, and it's what we wanted, us girls like being close."

"Well, we see you've met out husbands, and brothers."

"Yea, we did," said the group. "So, T.J., K.C. and D.J., do you three live here too?" asked Dante.

"No, we live across town in connecting houses also," said T.J.

"Oh, okay cool," said the group.

"Well now, how about we head on out to the backyard?" said Ashley.

"Okay sure." "Hey, listen we hope you don't mind but we've brought all kinds of cookout stuff and everything else that we would need for the day and night," said Dante.

"Great and thanks," said Ashley. "Yea sure, we were hoping to spend the rest of the day and evening with you all, we want to get to know you better," said the guest.

"Yea, we feel the same way," said Ashley and her siblings.

"Great." "Well now this is going to be interesting and fun," said the guests.

"Yea we should say so," said Ashley and her family.

CHAPTER 29

"Hey girls and guys, our guests are here," called Ashley.

A minute or two later the girls and guys came rushing down the stairs, "yay you all are here, we're so glad you could come," they said.

"Yea, us too," said the guests group.

"Well come on let's go have some fun," said the girls and guys.

"Yea sure, we're ready," said the guests.

CHAPTER 30

Before they knew it twelve o'clock was upon them, "wow look at the time it's late," said Ashley.

"Yea, I should say so, it's Tuesday morning already," said T.J.

"Yea, it is," said Dante. "Well, everyone it's been a blast, thanks again for having us."

"Yea sure, you're welcome, and we had fun too," said Ashley and her siblings.

"Great," Dante and his group said. "Well, we'd better be going now, maybe we'll see you tomorrow."

"Sure, that sounds like a plan, but if you're planning to come over, please make it after eleven," said Ashley.

"Oh okay, why though?" asked Dante.

"Well Chelsea, Madison and Harper all have doctor appointments at nine o'clock," said Ashley.

"Okay sure, no problem," said Dante. "Alright, well bye everyone we've enjoyed it."

"Yea, us too, well bye, and be careful," said Ashley and her family.

Ashley shut the door, and then turned around to the others, "wow that was a long day," Ashley said.

"Yea you can say that again, but it was fun," said Dante. "Well, we guys hate to rush off, but we all have to get up in a couple of hours."

"Alright, bye guys," Ashley and her siblings said.

"Yea bye girls," said the guys, and then they walked out the door.

After the guys had walked out the door, "well I don't know about the rest of you girls but I'm going to bed, I'm tired," said Ashley.

"Yea, we are too, so good night," said the girls.

"Yea, good night," came from Ashley.

CHAPTER 31

Chelsea, Harper and Madison were all up by seven getting ready for their doctor's appointments, when suddenly they heard footsteps coming closer and within seconds there standing in the doorway was Sarah, "What are you three girls doing up at this ungodly hour?"

"Well, we're getting ready for our doctor's appointments this morning," said Chelsea, Madison and Harper.

"Oh yea, that's right, thanks for reminding me, I'd forgotten all about that, and I'm sorry," said Sarah.

"Oh, don't be, it's alright, no big deal," said the girls.

"Okay whatever," said Sarah. "Give me thirty minutes to an hour and then I'll be ready to take you girls."

"Sure, no problem," said Chelsea, Madison and Harper.

Sarah smiled, "great."

CHAPTER 32

While the three girls were waiting on Sarah, they sat chatting about everything that had transpired over the whole weekend and week and what's to come.

CHAPTER 33

Forty-five minutes later Sarah walked into the room, "okay girls I'm ready to go," said Sarah.

"Alright," said the three, and so they stood up and following Sarah to the door.

As Sarah and her three younger sisters were walking out the door, the phone started ringing.

On the fourth ring Serena picked up answering, "hello."

"Hey Serena, it's mom," said Elaine.

"Oh, hey mom," said Serena." "So, what're you girls up to right now?" asked Elaine.

"Well, me I'm sleeping, I don't know about the others," said Serena.

"Oh okay, I'm sorry I woke you,"

said Elaine.

"No problem mom," said Serena.

"Good," said Elaine. "Well honey, I was just calling to check.

"Alright, well everything here's great," said Serena.

"Great, I'm glad to hear that," Elaine said.

"So, what about you and dad?" asked Serena.

"Well Dear, we are having the time of our lives," said Elaine.

"Great, that's great to hear," said Serena.

"Alright, well tell the rest of the clan that we called to check in and we love you girls," Elaine said.

"Okay, we love you too, and have fun," said Serena.

"Okay, you too, see you girls

Thursday or Friday but we're not sure which day yet though," said Elaine.

"Alright, yes ma'am, no problem," said Serena.

"Great, well bye Serena," said Elaine.

"Okay, yes ma'am, bye," said Serena, and then she hung up, and then went back to sleep.

CHAPTER 34

It was around eleven thirty when Sarah, Chelsea, Harper and Madison walked through the door, "wow that was a long doctor's appointments," said Harper.

"Yea, no doubt, and all because of the fifty million questions that Chelsea decided to ask," said Madison.

"Sorry but it helps to ask and know what's expected, and that's why you're supposed to ask questions," said Chelsea.

"Fine," said Madison. "Well anyway, it looks like we're right on schedule and we're around four months pregnant," said Chelsea. "Doctor Anderson said next month he'll be able to tell us what we're expecting."

"Oh wow, that's great news and so exciting," said Sarah.

"Yea, it is," said Chelsea. "Hey Sarah."

"Yea Chelsea," said Sarah. "Sarah, when Ashley and Serena get up, we really need to talk to you three about somethings," said Chelsea.

"Oh, sure no problem, that's what

we're here for," said Sarah.

"Great and thanks," said Chelsea. "Girls, say when are your boyfriends coming over?" asked Sarah.

"Well, Derek, Dante and Aaron will be here around lunchtime but due to Trevor,

Trenton and Gabe having jobs, the girls probably won't come today," said Chelsea.

"Oh okay," said Sarah. "So, girls when are your boyfriends getting jobs?"

"They're looking now," said Chelsea, Madison and Harper.

"Okay that's great to hear," said Sarah. "Well now let's get ready for your boyfriends to come over."

"Okay sure but that's what we kinda wanted to talk to you about," said Chelsea, Madison and Harper.

"Oh really," said Sarah. "Yea," said Chelsea.

"Well alright give me a few minutes and let me go get them," said Sarah.

"Sure," said Chelsea, Madison ands Harper.

CHAPTER 35

Ten minutes later here came Sarah, Serena and Ashley, "okay we understand that you three need to talk to us?"

"Yes," said Chelsea, Madison and Harper.

"Okay, so spill it," said Ashley. "Alright sure here it goes, well we have some concerns," said Chelsea,

Madison and Harper.

"Okay, no problem, everyone goes through that," said Ashley.

"Really?" "Seriously?" said Chelsea, Madison and Harper.

"Yea it's a natural feeling," said Ashley.

Chelsea stood up, "I'm speaking for us three," said Chelsea.

"Okay good," said Ashley. "Serena, Sarah, and Ashley first off we don't even know if want to get married, much less not being sure of being ready for marriage yet," said Chelsea. "It's one thing to be pregnant but dropping a marriage onto of this mess I'm afraid is too much to talk all in right now."

"Okay that's alright to have feelings like that, they're normal," said

Ashley. "Listen girls just because you're engaged doesn't mean you have to rush right into marriage right now or even this year."

"Oh really," said Chelsea. "Yea you see that engagement ring means you're promised to someone, but nothing is final yet," said Ashley.

"Oh okay, that's good to know," said Chelsea.

"Yea, it is," said Ashley. "So, girls, is there anything else?"

"Yes, we're concerned that the guys won't get jobs and therefore they won't be able to support their children let alone us," Chelsea said.

"Okay, listen right now I wouldn't worry about that and secondly you girls need to learn to depend on yourselves, don't ever depend on a man solely for anything you won't get anywhere in life if you depend on a man solely," said Ashley. "Girls, you need to let these guys prove themselves to you first before you settle."

"Oh okay, so basically what you're saying is for us to get jobs and support ourselves, our children and not worry about anything in less you have too," said Chelsea.

"Yes, that's what we're saying," said Ashley. "You girls are going to be alright."

"Yea, we hope so," said Chelsea. "You will be, we have faith in you girls, and plus we're here for you girls anytime day or night," said Ashley.

"Thank you so much, we feel better," said Chelsea.

"Great, we're glad," said Ashley. "Look girls it's nearing lunchtime, your boyfriends will be here any minute, so let's go get ready."

"Yeah, okay," said Chelsea, Madison and Harper.

CHAPTER 36

Fifteen minutes later a knock sounded at the door, "oh wow they're here," said Madison, and so Madison hurried over and opened the door and there stood Dante, Derek and Aaron.

"Hey girls," said Trevor, Trenton and Gabe.

"Hey guys," said Chelsea, Madison and Harper.

"Well come on in." "Thanks," said Trevor, Trenton and Gabe and so they started through the door, and for the next several hours the group of twelve had a blast, just enjoying the company, pool, cooking out and so much more.

CHAPTER 37

Before they knew it midnight rolled around, and everyone was wrapping up the huge fun day.

"Well, everyone it's been a blast but I'm afraid it's time for us to bounce," said Dante.

"It's late and we three have to get up in a few hours for work."

"Oh wow." "Really?" "Seriously?" said Chelsea. Madison and Harper.

"Yes, we three have jobs now," said Dante, Derek and Aaron.

"Wow, that's great congratulations," said Chelsea, Madison and Harper.

"Thanks, but seeing that we have families now that we have to take care of, it's a must," said Dante, Derek and Aaron.

"Wow that's awesome," said Chelsea, Madison and Harper.

"Yea, we think so," said Dante, Derek and Aaron.

"We really do love you girls and we really want to marry you girls soon."

"Wow that's nice to hear, we think," said Chelsea, Madison and Harper.

"Yea, thanks to your older brothers," said Dante, Derek and Aaron.

"Excuse us," said Chelsea, Madison and Harper. "What're you talking about exactly?"

"Well, you see the first night that we came over and met everyone in your family and that's also the same day that your older brothers pulled us aside and had a little talk with us," said Dante, Derek and Aaron.

"Oh really," said Chelsea, Madison and Harper.

"Yea and we're really glad that they had that little talk with us it shows us that they really care about you three, and that's a plus in our books," said Dante, Derek and Aaron.

"Okay great, we think," said Chelsea, Madison and Harper.

"Well girls we have to rush off but we three have to be up in a few hours," said Dante, Derek and Aaron.

"Okay sure, maybe we'll see you soon," Chelsea, Madison and Harper.

"Okay, well we'll keep in touch everyday," Dante, Derek and Aaron.

"Alright bye," said Chelsea, Madison and Harper.

After the three guys had left and Madison had shut the door, the six girls all looked at one another, "wow that's unbelievable our older brothers actually had a talk with our boyfriends," Madison said.

"Yea, uh actually to be technical they're our fiance's," said Chelsea.

"Yea whatever," said Madison. "Girls, I can't believe it either, but it looks like our boyfriends fiance's or whatever you want to call them they actually heeded our brothers talk."

"Yea, we know and it's great," said Harper.

"Yea, now I feel better about being with my chosen guy," said Chelsea.

"Yea, us too," said Madison and Harper.

"Great," said Chelsea. "Well, I don't know about you two but I'm tired, and I'm going to bed."

"Yea, us too, good night," said Madison and Harper.

"Yea, good night," said Chelsea.

CHAPTER 38

March fifteen Wednesday morning rolled around, the houses was quiet, due to everyone still fast asleep, when suddenly the phone started ringing

"On the fourth ring, Ashley reached up and snatched the phone off the cradle answering hello, hello."

"Hey dear, it's mom," said Elaine. "Oh, hey mom," said Ashley.

"What're you girls up too?" asked Elaine.

"Sleeping," said Sarah. "It's only seven."

"Oh okay, sorry we were jut calling to check in," said Elaine.

"So, how's everyone and everything?"

"Fine," said Sarah. "So, how's your trip?"

"Great," said Elaine. "Dear, by the way we'll be home Thursday."

"Oh okay, see you then," said Sarah. "Well, have fun."

"Thanks, and yea you too," said Elaine.

"Okay bye," said Sarah, and then she hung up, and then laid in the bed for another hour or so contemplating on what to do today.

CHAPTER 39

Eight fifteen rolled around and Sarah decided to get up and get ready for the day.

CHAPTER 40

Forty-five minutes later Sarah walked into the family room and found Ashley sitting on the couch writing in her notebook, "good morning Ashley," Ashley looked up, "oh good morning Sarah, I didn't hear you walk in," said Ashley.

"Hey mom and dad called this morning around seven," said Sarah.

"Yea, I heard the phone ring and I kind of figured it was them, so what did they have to say?" Ashley said.

"Nothing much but they've decided that their coming home Thursday," said Sarah.

"Excuse me tomorrow is Thursday," said Ashley.

"Oh jeez," said Sarah. "So Ashley, I was thinking, how about we call the guys and make plans to take these six back home and we stay there and make a weekend of it at mom and dads?"

"Yea sure that sounds great," said Ashley.

"Anyway, well let's get going," said Sarah.

"Yea sure," said Ashley. "I'll go get the other four."

"Alright, while you're doing that, I'm going to start making the calls to the guys," said Sarah.

"Okay great," said Ashely. "Uh Sarah, you do know that we're going to have to let our husbands know what our plans are."

"Yea, no duh, yuh think," said Sarah. "We will but first let's handle all this stuff."

CHAPTER 41

It was around ten thirty, "hey Ash." "Yea Sarah."

"I got ahold of the guys," said

Sarah.

"Oh good," said Ashley. "Yea their going to meet us at mom and dads around lunchtime," said Sarah.

"Okay great," said Ashley. Just then Serena, Chelsea, Madison and Harper walked into the family rooms loaded down with all kinds of bags and so forth, "wow that's a lot of stuff," said Ashley.

"Yea, we know," said Chelsea, Madison, Harper and Serena.

"Well, is everyone and everything ready to go?" asked Ashley.

"Yes," said Chelsea, Madison, Harper and Serena.

"Great." "Well alright then let's get ready and go," said Ashley.

"Sure," said Sarah. "Sarah and Serena, I just talked to our husbands," said Ashley.

"Oh yea," said Serena and Sarah. "Yea there's a change of plans," said Ashley.

"Oh okay, what kinda changes?" asked Serena and Sarah.

"Well, our husbands are going to meet us this afternoon with our children," Ashley said.

"Okay, that's great," said Sarah and Serena.

"Yea it is," said Ashley. "Well now let's get on the road already."

The girl clan smiled, "yes let's."

CHAPTER 42

Twelve on the dot, four cars pulled up in the driveways.

Minutes later everyone was

walking into the house, "okay you six need to go ahead and put your things away and call mom and dad let them know that you kids are home now but whatever you do don't tell them we're here with you kids," said Ashley.

"Okay, no problem, and we won't," said Chelsea, Madison, Harper, Trevor, Trenton and Gabe.

"Great." "Well, while you kids are handling that, we older ones are going to get settled," said Ashley.

"Okay sure," said Chelsea. "Wow this is going to be a very interesting visit."

"Yea to say the least," said Ashley.

CHAPTER 43

A couple of hours later Chelsea,

Madison, Harper, Trevor, Trenton and Gabe made their way back into the family room, "hey girls and guys, did you get everything taking care of?" asked Chelsea, and her siblings.

"Yea." "So, did you get in touch with mom and dad?" asked Ashley.

"Yea, we did," said Chelsea. "Okay, so what did they have to say?" asked Ashley.

"Nothing much, they wanted to know why we all came home early," said Chelsea.

"Alright, so what did you tell them?" asked Ashley.

"Well, we told them that we were ready to come and so we did," said Chelsea.

"Oh yea, they said they would be home tomorrow around lunchtime."

"Okay great," said Ashley. "Well then I have a suggestion."

"Okay, what?" asked Chelsea. "Well, why don't we have the whole house cleaned top to bottom, I mean everything all bathrooms, bedrooms, family room, den, dinning area and the kitchen," said Ashley.

"Okay sure, that's a great idea," said the younger siblings.

"Good." "Well let's get started," said Ashley.

CHAPTER 44

Before they knew it five o'clock was upon them and three cars pulled up in the driveway.

Minutes later a knock sounded at the door, and so Ashley hurried over and opened the door, "hey guys and kids, you finally made it," said Ashley.

"Yea, we're finally here," they said. "Good." "Well come on in," said Ashley.

CHAPTER 45

Chelsea, Madison, Harper, Trevor, Trenton and Gabe are getting ready to graduate high school in two months and their so excited that they can't wait but the group of six hiding one huge crazy secret from their parents that they've had since last summer and things are about to get really interesting when their parents get home from their trip this afternoon, to be exact less than an hour and on top of it all their siblings are stuck right slap in the middle of it.

CHAPTER 46

Twelve o'clock on the dot Elaine and Doug pulled into the driveway straight into the middle garage.

"Hey everyone mom and dad just pulled into the garage," said Chelsea.

"Oh really," said Ashley. "Yea," came from Chelsea, and so the older kids disappeared.

Minutes later Elaine and Doug came through the garage, making their way into the house, "hey kids, we're home," Elaine and Doug said.

Within minutes the kids came walking into the room, "hey mom and dad, welcome home," the kids said.

"Thanks," said Elaine and Doug.

"So, how was your trip?" asked Chelsea and her siblings.

"Great." "It was a lot of fun and really relaxing," said Elaine and Doug.

"Great, we're glad you two had a wonderful time, you two deserved it," said Chelsea and her siblings.

"Yea, we did," said Elaine and Doug. Just then Ashley, Damien, Serena, Chase, Sarah, Chris, T.J., K.C. and D.J. and all nine grandchildren came out from the hallway, "oh wow, what a surprise," said Elaine and Doug. "What're you all doing here?"

"Well, we decided to come spend the weekend here with the kids," said Ashley.

"Oh, okay that's a nice surprise," said Elaine and Doug.

"Yea, we thought so," said Ashley.

"Well, we're going to unload the car now and then get settled," said Elaine and Doug.

"Oh sure," said Ashley and the rest of the clan.

"Wait a minute mom and dad, us son in laws will go unload your car for you, while you go relax and enjoy your kids and grandkids," said Chris, Damien and Derek.

"Okay thanks, and that sounds great," said Elaine and Doug.

"Yea sure, no problem," said Chris, Chase and Damien.

When the guys had gone, Madison, Chelsea, Harper, Trenton, Trevor, and Gabe looked at their parents, "hey mom and dad."

"Yea kids," said Elaine and Doug. "Guess, what?" asked the group.

"What?" asked Elaine and Doug. "Well, the prom is coming up in less than three weeks," said Chelsea.

"Oh yea," said Elaine and Doug. "Yes ma'am, and sir," said Chelsea.

"Well, are you kids going?" asked Elaine and Doug.

"Yes ma'am, and sir, we're planning on it," said Chelsea.

"Okay good," said Elaine and Doug. Chelsea, Madison, Harper, Trenton, Trevor and Gabe smiled, "so we were wondering, when we can go shopping for prom attire?" asked Chelsea.

"Well then, how about Saturday morning?" Elaine asked.

"Alright, yes ma'am, that sounds great," said Chelsea.

"Great." "Saturday morning it is

then," said Elaine.

"Oh wow, thanks mom," said Chelsea, Harper and Madison.

"Yea sure, I'm looking forwards to some much-needed girl time," said Elaine.

CHAPTER 47

It's March seventh early Saturday morning, and Elaine and her three daughters are getting ready to go shopping for prom attire.

Elaine pushed the intercom button, "girls."

"Yes ma'am," the girls said. "I'm ready to go," Elaine said.

"Alright, yes ma'am we're coming, said Chelsea, Harper and Madison. "Good," said Elaine.

Minutes later the girls were walking into the kitchen, "mom this is going to be interesting and fun," said Chelsea, Harper and Madison.

"Yea, no doubt, yuh think," said Elaine. "Hey girls."

"Ma'am," said Chelsea, Harper and Madison.

"Did you happen to ask your older sisters?" asked Elaine.

"Yes, and they declined they want to stay home and relax but they said they might meet us for lunch," said Chelsea, Harper and Madison. "Okay great," said Elaine.

As the four ladies headed out the door, Elaine was out in front of them, Ashley leaned over and whispered to Chelsea, "we can't keep lying to them," said Ashley.

"Yes, I know this, so what do we do?" asked Chelsea.

"I don't know yet," said Ashley. "Okay." "Well, I say let's just go along with this mom and daughters shopping day," said Chelsea.

"Yea sure, that works for us," said Ashley and Harper.

"Great," Chelsea.

CHAPTER 48

Chelsea, Madison and Harper met three cut boys at last year's summer camp and they've been secretly dating and keeping in touch with these three boys for a year now, and all the while lying and hiding everything from their parents but now each one has a huge disturbing secret and they don't have clue what they're going to do much less what they're going to say and then on top of it their older siblings are stuck slap dab right in the middle.

CHAPTER 49

Elaine and the girls got in the van, "well girls are you ready to go?" asked Elaine.

"Yea, we guess," came from the three.

"Good," said Elaine, and while Elaine had the music turned up, the girls huddled together, "alright well girls, should we talk to her now or later?" Madison.

"Well, I think we should feel her out first," said Chelsea.

"Okay that's a great idea

Chelsea," said Madison.

"Thanks," said Chelsea. "If it's alright with you two I'll be the spokesperson for us."

"Yea sure," said Madison and Harper.

"Great." "Well alright then, here we go, "hey mom," said Chelsea.

"Yea Chelsea," said Elaine. "Mom, I have a hypothetical question for you."

"Oh yea," said Elaine. "Yes ma'am," said Chelsea.

"Alright, I'm ready," said Elaine. "Okay great," said Chelsea. "Well hypothetically speaking what would you do if one of your daughters or sons came to you with a massive problem?"

"Well Chelsea dear,

hypothetically speaking I would do my best to be understanding and helping in fixing it no matter what the problem or issue," said Elaine.

"Oh wow." "Really?" "Seriously?" said Chelsea.

"Yea there's nothing I wouldn't so for anyone of my kids no matter how bad or how big the problem," said Chelsea.

"Oh wow, that's great to know," said Chelsea.

"Yea," said Elaine. "Alright mom we're ready to go shopping now," said Chelsea.

"Great," said Elaine, and then the girls went back to talking amongst themselves, all the while just sat there shaking her head and thinking to herself how weird that was.

A few minutes later, "hey girls we're here," said Elaine.

"Okay great," said Chelsea and Madison.

"Whatever," said Harper. "Let's go so we can get this over with," said Harper.

"Okay, whatever Harper," said Chelsea and Madison, all the while Elaine ignoring her daughter Harper's complaining and snide remarks, "well come on the sooner we get started, the sooner we get done and then we can get out of here," said Elaine.

"Alright, yes ma'am," said Harper, Madison and Chelsea.

"You know girls this isn't my idea of a fun weekend haven to shop with you three for prom attire not to mention all the money that I'm having to put out for all three of you.”

“Listen if you girls don’t want to do all this shopping today then I guess you don’t want to go to the prom very bad,” said Elaine.

“Mom, we do want to go to the prom, we’re sorry,” said Chelsea, Madison and Harper.

“Alright then let’s go shopping and get this over with, and Harper I don’t want to hear another complaint or snide comment from you,” said Elaine.

“Yea alright whatever,” said Harper.

“Good,” said Elaine.

CHAPTER 50

By lunchtime the four ladies were

hungry and loaded down with shopping bags, "so girls, what do we want for lunch?" asked Elaine.

"How about Italian?" said Chelsea. "Great that sounds good," said Elaine.

CHAPTER 51

Fifteen minutes later the four ladies were sitting down at a round table, "well girls I must say I'm really happy with the choices that you all have chosen," said Elaine.

"Thanks," said Chelsea, Madison and Harper, all the while all three girls were rolling their eyes.

"Look girls you all are going to look very beautiful for your dates," said Elaine.

"Thanks mom," said the three. "Yea and I'm pretty sure your dates have your whole prom night all planned out."

"Oh yea, we're sure they do," said the three.

"Now girls I can't tell you how very proud I am of all three of you, you all have out done yourselves with outstanding grades, sports and everything else."

"You all will go far in life, I'm just so happy that you three didn't take the wrong road and get mixed up with a coupled of bad idiot choices for friends in the boy department." "I have to say that you all have surprised me by not getting involved with any kind of so-called boys unlike your older sisters."

"I know it must be hard for you."
"I was young once to and I even made many mistakes in the boy department, but I made it through the teenage drama years, and later on when I actually grew up that's when I met my soulmate who was meant for me and believe it or not your three older sisters even met their true soulmates when they were your age but only by accident and with issues," said Elaine. "Girls bottom line is everything happens for a reason whether it was a mistake or not," said Elaine.

"Oh wow, thanks mom," said Chelsea, Madison and Harper.

"Yea sure, you're welcome," said Elaine.

Chelsea stood up, "come on Harper and Madison let's go to the bathroom for a minute," said Chelsea.

"Okay sure but why though?" said Madison.

"Well, if you must know I need to use the restroom, check my hair and so forth," said Chelsea.

"Oh okay, yea us too," said Madison and Harper. "Mom, excuse us we'll be right back."

"Sure girls, no problem," said Elaine, and then her girls got up and started walking away.

While Elaine was waiting on her three daughters to get back, she started thinking to herself I know my girls are up to something, they're hiding something but what whatever it is it can't be good.

CHAPTER 52

"Oh my, gosh this can't be happening," said Chelsea.

"Yea, we know this, so what do we do, how do we go about this?" Madison and Harper.

"Well, I guess we need to go ahead and break the news to her now about everything," said Chelsea.

"Yea okay," said Madison and Harper. "Well let's do this and get it over with."

"Okay," said Chelsea. "Well, this is just going to be lovely."

"Yea, no doubt," said Madison and Harper, and so the three girls walked out of the bathroom heading back to where their mom sat.

Minutes later they sat down, "hey mom."

"Yes girls," said Elaine. "Mom,"

we have something to talk to you about," said Chelsea.

"Oh yea," said Elaine. "Yes ma'am, but it's more like a confession," said Chelsea.

"Uh huh really?" said Elaine. "Yes ma'am, and this isn't going to be easy," said Chelsea.

"Uh huh well, what is it?" Elaine asked.

"Mom, I'm speaking for all of us and mind you this is very hard, so please bear with me," said Chelsea.

"Sure," said Elaine. "Alright, well here goes nothing," said Chelsea, and then she took a couple of deep calming breaths, and then she said, "mom all six of us have been lying, and hiding a huge secret from you and dad since last summer," said Chelsea.

"Uh huh, wow I can't believe this," said Elaine. "No, I take that back, I can because I suspected that you six were hiding something from us but wasn't sure what exactly." "Alright go on spill it."

"Yes ma'am," said Chelsea. "Well, we kinda met three guys last year and we've been dating and keeping in touch with them."

"Uh huh, I knew it," said Elaine, and she sat there for a minute with her head in her hands and then she looked back up, "so let me get this straight you girls and boys have been lying and hiding these boyfriends and girlfriends for about a year now without us knowing this."

"Yes ma'am, we're sorry for everything we made a mistake,

granite a big one," said Chelsea.

"Oh yea, I should say so," Elaine said. "So, girls, why didn't you just come to us and be up front and truthful about everything?"

"We don't know we guess we were to scared and ashamed to come to you and dad," said Chelsea, Madison and Harper.

"Oh yea." "Really?" "Seriously?" "Why?" asked Elaine.

"Well maybe because we knew what we were doing wrong but we wanted to hang out with these people and get to know them better we care about them and we want them in our lives," said Chelsea. "Mom, we're sorry for everything we didn't mean to cause any trouble, we made mistake granite a big one."

"Yea, no doubt, I should say so," said Elaine. "Girls, I don't mind telling you very mad upset and very disappointed in kids, I just can't for the life of me understand why you just didn't come to me in the first place instead of here."

"Sorry mom," said Chelsea. "Yea whatever," said Elaine.

"Well girls I say we go home for the night."

"Yea sure," said Chelsea, Madison and Harper.

As they were getting into the car, Elaine looked back at her three girls with hurt in her face, "thank you girls for telling me this and for finally being up front with me about this whole horrific situation," said Elaine.

"Now girls, is there anything else

that I should know about before we get home?"

"Yes ma'am," said Chelsea. "Mom we all wrote notes to you and dad telling, more less explaining everything about this whole horrible mess."

"Great, I can't wait to read them," said Elaine.

"Okay, yea us too," said Chelsea.

CHAPTER 53

Fifteen minutes later Elaine and the girls were walking through the front door loaded down with all kinds of shopping bags, "hey babe and girls."

"Hey honey," said Elaine. "So, how was the shopping trip and girl time?" Doug asked.

"Real interested," said Elaine. "Oh really?" said Doug. "Yes really," said Elaine. "Everyone family meeting now."

"Okay, yes ma'am," said the clan. "Yea, alright honey, what's going on?" Doug asked.

"You'll know soon enough," said Elaine.

CHAPTER 54

Once everyone was seated, Elaine stood up in front of her huge family, "alright everyone it's been brought to my attention that Chelsea, Madison, Harper, Trevor, Trenton and Gabe, you six have been lying hiding and going behind our backs about several things since last summer, so before I go any further, who else knew about this huge horrible mess?" said Elaine. Suddenly Sarah, Serena, Ashley, T.J., K.C., D.J., Chase, Chris and Damien put their hands.

"Oh wow." "Oh my, gosh this can't be happening," said Elaine.

"So let me, ask you something, why didn't you come straight to us?" said Elaine.

Ashley stood, "well mom and dad when we found out about this you two were gone on your trip," said Ashley.

"Oh really," said Elaine. "Yes ma'am, and we didn't want to bother you so we thought we could handle this on our own and for the most part we did," said Ashley.

"Okay." "Well thank you for thinking of us, that was very sweet of you all," said Elaine.

"Yes ma'am, you're welcome," said Ashley.

"Alright kids, I know you six have written notes to us, so please go ahead and give them to me," said Elaine.

"Yes ma'am," said Ashley, and so Ashley stood up and walked over and handed them to her, "here you go mom."

"Thanks Ashley," said Elaine. "Yes ma'am, you're welcome," Ashley said.

"Alright everyone we're going to go talk things over and then we'll be back to tell you all what we're going to do," said Elaine.

"Yes ma'am, and sir," said the

clan, and then Elaine and Doug let the room.

Minutes later the door slammed shut.

CHAPTER 55

"Honey, I can't believe this they're following in their older sister's footsteps," said Elaine.

"Ah, yea it looks that way," said Doug.

"Doug, you know something we didn't have any kinda trouble out of K.C., D.J. and T.J.," said Elaine.

"Yea, I know but babe they were the shy ones that didn't put themselves out there in the middle of everyone or everything," said Doug.

"Yea, you're right," said Elaine.

"So, what are we going to do?"

"I don't know yet, but I do know this I don't want to have to raise anymore babies," said Doug.

"Yea you've got a point me either, but I have to say I've enjoyed every minute of raising the ones that we've been blessed with," said Elaine.

"Yes dear, me too," said Doug. "Well let's go ahead and read over these letters and see what we're looking at and then we'll have a better idea of the mess that they've manage to get themselves in."

"Yea that sounds like a good idea," said Elaine.

"Great," said Doug.

CHAPTER 56

For the next thirty minutes to an hour all eighteen kids of all ages sat around talking spending time quality time together while waiting for their parents to come back into the family room.

CHAPTER 57

Before they realized it the bedroom door had opened up, and Elaine and Doug were making their way back down the hallway towards the family room, "hey everyone, look they're coming back now," said Serena.

"Oh wow." "Oh my, gosh," said Sarah. "Well let's just hope they're not mad or upset."

"Yea we can only hope," said

Ashley.

"Yea isn't that the truth," Sarah said.

"Alright kids we've read your letters, and we've talked it over and this is what we're going to do," said Elaine.

"Okay, what?" asked Chelsea. "Well, you six girls will be here in the family room, and boys you will be with your dad," said Elaine.

"Okay, yes ma'am and sir," the girls and guys said.

"Well come on boys we're going to the basement," said Doug.

"Yes sir," said the guys, and then the boys stood up and started walking out of the room.

As soon as the guys had left the room, Elaine then looked at every girl sitting down in the family room for several minutes, and then said, "girls you should know I'm very mad, upset, and just plain hurt about this whole ugly situation," said Elaine.

"Yea, we know," said the girls. "Good," said Elaine.

"Mom we're sorry about everything, we didn't mean to make you mad, hurt or even make you upset that wasn't our intentions at all and we kinda just got ourselves into a huge mess and didn't know what to do," Chelsea said. "Mom, we made a mistake, granite a huge one but nevertheless a mistake."

"Yea, I should say so," said Elaine. "Mom, we're just human things happen," Chelsea said.

"Yea, I know all this but it still

doesn't excuse any of this or any of you just so you know," said Elaine.

"Yes ma'am, we understand," said Chelsea.

"Good," said Elaine. "Now Chelsea, Madison and Harper I'm going to go ahead and tell you right now that I'm made at you three but I'm even madder at you three older ones Serena, Sarah and Ashley for hiding this horrific mess from me and your dad."

"Yea we know and we're sorry mom, but we thought we we're doing the right thing by try to handle this huge mess on our own, we just wanted you and dad to just have a fun week without any worries and concerns," said Ashley.

"Well, I thank you girls and I must

say that you for the most part have done a great job of working on this horrific mess with your younger sisters and brothers," said Elaine.

"Thanks, we think, we did alright considering the mess, and besides we've seen you in work mode enough that we just followed code," said Ashley.

Elaine smiled, "great."

CHAPTER 58

"Guys, I can't tell you or explain to you six how made at you I am," said Doug.

"Yea we can imagine, and we're sorry dad," said Trenton, Trevor, Gabe, T.J., K.C. and D.J.

"Yea, I know," said Doug. "Guys, I

must say this is some kinda mess you three have gotten yourselves into and not to mention that you three older ones were the helpers and cleaners of this horrific mess."

"Well now Trenton, Trevor and Gabe you three do realize and understand that your teenage years are over as you know it."

"Yes sir, we know," said Trevor, Trenton and Gabe.

"Alright then," said Doug. "Dad just so you know we have jobs, we're still in high school, we plan to graduate and still go along with our college career plans," said Trevor, Trenton and Gabe.

"Wow that's great to hear," said Doug.

"Yea but there's more dad," said

Trevor.

"Alright go ahead," said Doug. "Well Dad we plan on marrying these three girls and raising our own children," said Trevor, Trenton and Gabe.

"Wow alright," said Doug. "Well then in that case I think you're on the right path." "Wow you three guys are growing up right in front of my eyes." "Guys, I'm so proud of you three for the men that you guys are becoming to be and most importantly for stepping up and doing the right thing."

"Thanks dad," said Trevor, Trenton and Gabe.

"Yea, you're welcome," said Doug.

CHAPTER 59

"Girls, I need to know your plans," said Elaine.

"Okay, but what do you mean exactly?" asked Chelsea.

"Well, I mean, are you going to raise these children or are dad and I going to get stuck with raising them?" Elaine said.

"Mom we're engaged to be married to these guys," said Chelsea.

"Oh wow," said Elaine. "Yes ma'am, and so to answer your question yes we're going to raise our own children," said Chelsea.

"Oh wow." "Oh my, gosh, I don't believe it," said Elaine.

"Alrighty then," said Chelsea. "Mom, don't worry we're going to graduate from high school, and we're planning on getting married sometime in early May before the babies actually come and definitely before graduation."

"Oh, and by the way we're all planning on getting jobs and we're still planning on going to college in the fall."

"Oh wow, you girls have really thought everything through," Elaine said.

"Yes ma'am, we have," said Chelsea.

"Wow, I must say besides being mad and upset at you girls, you girls have really made me so proud of you," said Elaine.

"Great that's what we were aiming for," said Chelsea.

Elaine smiled, "you three are

growing up right before my eyes."

"Thanks mom," said Chelsea, Madison and Harper.

"Yea, you're welcome," said Elaine.

"Well, jeez girls we have less than two months to get everything planned, and you girls didn't give me and your dad much time."

"Yes ma'am, we know, we're sorry," said Chelsea, Madison and Harper. "Anyway, say girls, I'm wondering something, when do we get to meet these three gentlemen that are about to be part of the family?" said Elaine.

"Anytime, just say the word," said Chelsea.

"Okay well, how about today?" said Elaine.

"Okay sure, we'll see what we can do," said Chelsea, Madison and Harper. "Great," said Elaine, and then the girls headed out of the room.

When the girls were out of sight, Elaine pulled out her phone and dialed Doug's number.

Within minutes his voice came through the line, "hello."

"Hey honey," said Elaine. "Hey babe, what's up?" said Doug.

"Nothing much, I'm just calling to let you know that you guys can come back up now," said Elaine.

"Okay great, we're on our way up now, we'll see you in a few minutes," said Doug.

"Okay great," said Elaine.

CHAPTER 60

"Wow honey, it looks like we're getting ready to add to our already extended family," said Elaine.

"Yea, I'm afraid so and it looks like we're going to be busy from here on out, first with prom right around the corner, then six weddings to plan for, graduation to plan for and not to mention the dozen or so new babies to get ready for also," said Doug.

"Jeez isn't that the truth," said Elaine.

"Mom and dad we have an idea," said Chelsea.

"Okay, what?" Elaine and Doug asked.

"Well, you see we were thinking, why don't we six get married on the first Friday of May at the curt-house and then maybe later on we all can have regular weddings maybe," said Chelsea.

"Yea alright that's good idea," said Elaine and Doug.

"Great," said Chelsea and her siblings. "We kid's just want to make things easy on you."

"Well, thanks for thinking of us," said Elaine and Doug.

"Sure," said Chelsea and her siblings.

"Mom, and dad you wanted to meet our boyfriends and girlfriends."

"Yes, we want to meet them," said Elaine and Doug.

"Great because they're on their way here now," said Chelsea and her siblings.

"Great, we can't wait," said Elaine and Doug.

"Yea, us either," said Chelsea, and her siblings.

CHAPTER 61

Twenty minutes later a black van pulled into the driveway, "hey mom, dad, and everyone, they're here," said Chelsea. "Great," came from everyone.

Minutes later a knock sounded at the door, and so they all hurried over to the door, "are we ready?"

"Yes," came from the group. "Okay," said Madison, and so she quickly opened the door and there stood six young people, "hey everyone, come in," said Madison. "Thanks," said the guests.

A minute or two later after

everyone was inside, "mom and dad, please meet our boyfriends Dante Eastland, Derek Crowder and Aaron Garrison," said Madison.

"Well, gentlemen it's really nice too finally meet you three," said Elaine and Doug.

"Yes ma'am, and sir, it's really nice to meet you folks also," said Dante, Derek and Aaron.

"Alright our turn, Mom, dad and everyone please meet our girlfriends Erin Deaton, Jana Peterson and Deanne Camps," said Trevor.

"Well ladies it's really nice to finally meet you three," said Elaine and Doug.

"Yes ma'am, and sir, it's really nice to finally meet you folks also," said Eric, Jana and Deanne.

"Well come on in let's go visit in the family room," said Elaine and Doug.

"Sure," said the group, and for the next several hours the group sat around talking, visiting getting to know one another.

CHAPTER 62

Around ten o'clock Doug looked at the clock, "jeez look at the time, it's late," said Doug.

"Yes sir, and yes ma'am, we all have to get up for work," said Dante.

"Yea, me too," said Doug. "Well, it was really nice to meet you folks," said Dante, Derek, Aaron, Erin, Jana and Deanne.

"Yea it's really nice meeting you

kids," said Elaine and Doug. "Well, we'll have to do this again soon."

"Yes ma'am, and sir, we would like that and we're looking forward to it," said Dante, Derek, Aaron, Erin, Jana and Deanne.

"Great, us too," said Doug and Elaine.

"Well, we hate to rush off, but we need to be going now we all have to get up early for work," said Dante, Derek, Aaron, Jana, Erin and Deanne.

"Yea, we understand that, bye," said Elaine and Doug. "Yea bye," the guests said.

As soon as the black van had left the driveway, Elaine and Doug turned to face their kids, "wow that seemed to go very well and they seem like really nice people too," said Elaine and

Doug.

"Yea, they are," said the girls. "Well now, I don't know about you kids, but we're tired this has been a very long day, "said Doug and Elaine.

"Yea it has and yea we're tired too," said the clan, and so Elaine, Doug and their kids headed to their respected rooms.

CHAPTER 63

April twenty third, five o'clock Friday morning rolled around, and everyone was up getting ready for the day.

CHAPTER 64

Around six thirty a.m. the kids

were making their way into the kitchen, "oh wow, I can't believe it our prom is upon us already," said Chelsea.

"Yea, we know, it's like tomorrow," said Harper.

"Yea, no doubt," said Madison.

"Well, I for one can't wait," Chelsea said.

"Yea Chelsea, we know us too," said Madison and Harper.

"Oh my, gosh, what are you girls so happy ad gabby this morning?" asked Trevor, Trenton and Gabe.

"Duh, tomorrow night is our prom," said Chelsea, Madison and Harper.

"Great." "Whoo hoo," said Trevor, Trenton and Gabe.

"Okay, what's wrong with you

guys this morning?" asked Chelsea, Madison and Harper.

"Nothing," they mumbled. "Uh huh."

"Okay, whatever you say," said Chelsea, Madison and Harper.

"Alright girls, I'll call the hair salon today and make you three appointments for early Saturday morning," said Elaine.

"Okay and thanks mom," said the girls.

"Yea sure, no problem," said Elaine.

As the kids were eating, Trevor called out, "hey mom."

"Yes son," said Elaine. "Mom, we three were wondering if you could find us some suits or whatever to wear for the prom?" Trevor said.

"Yea sure, I'll do my best," said Elaine.

"Great and thanks mom," said the guys.

"Yea sure, no problem," said Elaine.

CHAPTER 65

"Girls, oh my, gosh I can't believe it we have two more weeks until we get married," said Chelsea.

"Yea and just think a couple of weeks later we graduate high school," said Madison.

"Yea, we know and then soon after we'll have our babies," said Harper.

"Oh jeez, you're right and I for one I can't wait," said Chelsea.

"Yea, us too," said Madison and Harper.

"Well so far this year has been very interesting," said Chelsea.

"Yea you can say that again," said Madison.

CHAPTER 66

Thirty minutes later all six kids were going out the door.

As soon as they were gone, Elaine hurried into her bedroom to finish getting ready for her busy day, she had so many things to do today that she's not sure she'll get them all done but she would do her best to finish everything.

CHAPTER 67

Elaine was out the door thirty minutes later heading first to the mall to do her son's shopping and then from there she would handle the rest of her errands.

CHAPTER 68

She arrived home a little after four p.m.

Minutes later Elaine walked into the house straight through to the family room where she found all six of her kids sitting on the couches watching television, "hey kids, I'm home."

"Hey mom," they said. "Wow you were gone all day," said her kids.

"Yea, I had a lot to do today," Elaine said. "Guys, I found your prom attire.”

"Oh wow, thanks," said the guys.
"Yea sure," said Elaine.
"Well come look at them, see if you like everything I picked out."

"Okay, yes ma'am, we're coming," said the guys.

"Alright girls, I made you three hair appointments for eight o'clock in the morning," Elaine said.

"Okay thanks," said the girls. "Yea sure, you're welcome," said Elaine, and so she walked over to where her three sons were standing, "oh wow mom these are great, you did a good job, thank you so much," said her sons.

Elaine smiled, "oh you guys are so welcome, but you know I had to go to five stores to find everything."

"Wow, we're sorry you had to go through all that trouble," said the guys.

"Yea, well it was worth it, you only get to go to your senior prom once," said Elaine.

"Yea, we know," said her three sons.

Elaine smiled, and for the rest of the afternoon and night went by fast.

CHAPTER 69

Before they knew it Saturday morning was upon them.

Elaine pushed the intercom button for the girls room, "hey girls."

A minute or two later, "yes," came through.

"It's seven o'clock, you girls need

to be getting up now, you all have eight o'clock hair appointments this morning," said Elaine.

"Okay, we'll be down shortly," they said.

"Alright but hurry up," said Elaine. "Okay, yes ma'am," came through, Elaine then went about her business of getting everyone's prom outfits out, and ready for them later on this afternoon.

CHAPTER 70

Twenty minutes later her three daughters emerged from their bedrooms heading to the family room, "hey mom, we're ready to go, when you are," they said. "Okay great," said Elaine.

Minutes later Elaine and her three daughters were getting into the car and soon after they were heading to the salon hair shop.

CHAPTER 71

Four hours later the girls and Elaine were walking out of the salon, and soon after they were back in the van and heading home.

CHAPTER 72

After a twenty minute ride back home, they were finally walking back into the house, when Elaine heard, "mom."

"Yea son," said Elaine. "Mom, we have to pick up our dates at five o'clock due to having six o'clock reservations at Barabba's Italian Restaurant," said Trenton.

"Oh wow, that's great," said Elaine. "Yea, we think so," said her son.

"So, girls, where's your dinner reservations?" asked Elaine.

"Well mom it seems that we have reservations at the same place Barabba's," said the girls.

"Oh wow, well how did you all manage that?" asked Elaine.

"Well to be honest we're not sure but it's alright," said her daughters.

CHAPTER 73

Three o'clock rolled around and the girls and boys were getting ready for their special exciting nights.

CHAPTER 74

Four fifteen rolled around and the guys made their way into the family room first for their mom and dad's approval, "hey mom and dad, what do you think?" asked their sons.

"Oh wow, you three look absolutely handsome," said Elaine and Doug.

"Thanks," the guys said. "Yea sure, you're welcome," said Elaine and Doug.

"Now guys let me get some pictures before you all have to leave."

"Okay but hurry up," the guys said. "Yea sure," said Elaine.

A few minutes later the guys were

leaving out the door, as the girls were making their way into the family room for their mom and dad's approval, "hey mom and dad, how do we look?" the girls asked.

"Oh wow, you girls look absolutely beautiful," said Elaine and Doug.

"Chelsea that dark blue floor length dress, and matching shoes, and accessories looks absolutely gorgeous." "Derek is going to fall over himself."

"Thanks mom and dad," said Chelsea.

"Yea sure, you' re welcome," said Elaine.

"Madison, I must say that silver sequin floor length dress, matching shoes and accessories is absolutely stunning on you, Aaron's going to fall all over himself," said Elaine.

"Thanks mom and dad," said Madison.

"Yea sure, you're welcome," said Elaine.

"Wow Harper, that dark green floor length gown, matching shoes and accessories looks simply amazing on you, Dante's going to fall over himself," said Elaine.

"Thanks mom and dad," said Harper.

"Yea sure, you're welcome," said Elaine.

"Well now girls let me get some pictures before your dates get here."

"Okay sure but make it quick," said the girls.

"Okay great," said Elaine.

CHAPTER 75

Five o'clock on the dot a knock sounded at the door, Elaine and Doug walked over to the door and quickly opened it up and there stood the three guys Dante, Derek and Aaron who their daughters have chosen for their partners.

"Hey guys," said Doug and Elaine. "Hey Mr. and Mrs. Hollingsworth," the guys said.

"Wow you guys look great," said Elaine and Doug.

"Thanks," said the guys. "Well now, are you ready to see your girls?" asked Elaine and Doug.

"Yes ma'am, and sir, we are," said the guy.

"Good," said Elaine and Doug, and then they stepped out of the way and let the boys inside, "wow you girls look amazingly beautiful," the guys said.

"Thanks, and you guys look handsome also," said the girls.

"Thanks," said the guys. "Okay kids, let me get some pictures before you go," said Elaine.

"Okay, yes ma'am but please hurry," said the girls.

"Sure, no problem," said Elaine.

CHAPTER 76

Ten minutes later, the group of six were walking out the door for their special evening.

As soon as they were gone, Doug

and Elaine looked at one another, "wow they all looked so good," said Elaine.

"Yea, I know," said Doug. "Honey everyone's gone for the night," said Elaine.

"Yea, I know, and I can't believe it," Elaine said.

"Yea, me either we actually have the whole evening and night to ourselves, so what do you say we take advantage of it and spend the evening together for some much needed relaxing and enjoying each-others company while we have it," said Doug.

"Yea sure, that sounds wonderful," said Elaine.

Doug smiled, "great." Elaine smiled back, "yea it's great."

CHAPTER 77

Around one thirty the group of six walked in the door, "hey mom and dad, we're home."

"Hey kids," they said. "So, how was your evening?"

"It was wonderful, we had a lot of fun but right now we're all tired, we're going to bed," the kids said.

"Okay sure, talk to you kids later," said Elaine and Doug.

"Yea sure, good night," said the kids.

"Yea, good night kids," said Elaine and Doug.

CHAPTER 78

May fifth, Wednesday morning

rolled around, and everyone is up getting ready for the day.

"Wow, I can't believe we have only two more days until we get married," said Chelsea.

"Yea, we know," said Madison and Harper.

"Hey girls we need to go shopping for a couple of cute outfits for Friday," said Chelsea.

"Okay, yea you're right," said Madison and Harper.

"Say, how about we ask mom to go with us?" asked Chelsea.

"Yea sure, that's a great idea," said Madison and Harper.

"Well come on," said Chelsea, and so they stood up and headed out the door.

Minutes later the girls walked into

the kitchen, "hey mom."

"Yea girls," said Elaine. "Mom we were wondering, would you like to go shopping with us today?" asked Chelsea.

"Yea sure, that sounds fun," said Elaine. "By the way what're we going shopping for anyway?"

"Well, we wanted to go look for some cute wedding outfits and accessories," said Chelsea.

"Oh, okay great," said Elaine. "So, when do you want to leave?"

"Soon," said the girls." "Like in the next ten or fifteen minutes."

"Sure, I'll be ready to go," said Elaine.

"Great," said the girls.

CHAPTER 79

Fifteen minutes later Elaine walked out of her bedroom making her way down the hallway heading straight for the family room calling, "girls I'm ready when you three are."

"Okay, yes ma'am, coming," they called out.

Within minutes Elaine and her daughters were walking out the door.

CHAPTER 80

Seven o'clock rolled around and the ladies pulled into the driveway straight into the first garage, and soon after Elaine and the girls exited the suv and started grabbing their bags and soon after they were starting through the garage door.

Within minutes Doug was walking

towards them, "hey ladies."

"Hey guys," the ladies said. "Well let me help you ladies with these shopping bags," said Doug.

"Thanks that would be nice," said Elaine.

"Yea sure, no problem," said Doug. "So, how was your shopping trip?"

"It was wonderful," said Elaine and her girls.

"Good, I'm glad," said Doug. "Well, did you girls find everything that you needed?"

"Yes sir, we did," said the girls. "In fact, we actually got two outfits a piece with matching shoes and accessories."

"Wow, that's great," said Doug. "Yes sir, we agree," said the girls.

"Thanks mom."

"Yea sure, you girls are welcome," said Elaine, and then the girls were heading off towards their bedrooms.

"Wow honey, I can't believe it our second set of six are getting married Friday, and then their graduating from high school three weeks later and not to mention that soon after they all will be parents," said Elaine

"Yea, I know I can't believe it either," said Doug.

"Jeez so far this year has proved to be quite interesting," said Elaine.

"Yea, no doubt you can say that again," said Doug.

"Honey, I can't help but wonder what's coming next," said Elaine.

"Yea, no doubt but I'm not sure yet but whatever it is it's going to be a dossier," said Doug.

"Yea, I'm afraid you're right," said Elaine.

"Honey, you know I'm going to have to take the boys shopping tomorrow for their wedding attire."

"Yea, I know, have fun with that," said Doug.

"Yea thanks, ha ha very funny," said Elaine.

"Yea sure, anytime and yea you're welcome," said Doug.

Elaine pushed in the intercom button for the boys room and within seconds her son's voices came through, "yes ma'am."

"Boys I'm just letting you know that tomorrow morning we're going shopping for your wedding and graduation attire," said Elaine.

"Ah, man sure whatever," said the boys.

She quickly clicked off, "wo that went over real well, Elaine mumbled to herself.

"Yea it sounded like it," said Doug. "Babe, listen I have a better idea."

"Okay, what?" asked Elaine. "Well instead of dragging the boys off shopping for the day, why don't you go do the shopping for them by yourself or take the girls with you?" said Doug.

"Wow, yea that's a great idea," said Elaine.

"Great," said Doug. "Well in that case, I might just go tonight and get it over with," said Elaine.

"Yea sure, whatever you want to

do, it's fine with me," Doug said.

"Great," said Elaine, and Elaine pushed in the intercom for the girl's room.

Within minutes her daughter's voices came through, "yes ma'am."

"Girls, I was wondering, would you three like to go back shopping tonight with me?" asked Elaine.

"Yea sure, what for?" asked the girls.

"Well, I have to go find your three brothers two outfits a piece," said Elaine.

"Okay sure, we'll go with you and help," said her girls.

"Great," said Elaine. "So, when do you want to go?" asked the girls.

"Now," said Elaine. "Okay great, we're ready to go," said the girls.

"Good," said Elaine. "Honey, we ladies are off shopping again for the second time."

"Okay, well have fun," said Doug. "Yea we will, see you later," said Elaine.

"Okay bye," said Doug. "Yea bye," said Elaine.

CHAPTER 81

Elaine Pulled into the garage around midnight.

As they were exciting the over filled suv, when suddenly the garage door opened up, and there walking through was Doug.

"Hey ladies, I see you're finally home," said Doug. "So, how was your second shopping trip?" "Did you find everything that you were looking for?”

“It was great, we had a lot of fun and yes we found everything that we were going for,” said Elaine.

“Great,” said Doug. “Yea, I just hope the boys like the two outfits that we girls picked out for them,” said Elaine.

“Oh babe, I’m sure they will,” said Doug.

“Okay, I hope so,” said Elaine. “Yea, we hope you’re right dad,” said the girls.

“Yea, me too,” said Doug.

CHAPTER 82

Before everyone knew it, Friday morning was upon them.

“Oh my, gosh, wow Doug this is

the most exciting day of our six kids lives," said Elaine.

"Yea, I know, and I can't believe it's already upon us," said Doug.

"Yea, no doubt, well come on let's go get ready," said Elaine.

CHAPTER 83

A couple of hours later Elaine and Doug were sitting in the kitchen, when their son's Trevor, Trenton and Gabe entered the room, "hey mom and dad," they said.

"Hey guys," said Elaine and Doug. "Wow you three guys look great."

"Thanks," said the guys. "Mom, we must say you did a fantastic job of picking out our outfits."

"Thank you, I'm glad you like

them but to be honest I wasn't sure if you three would or wouldn't, and so I'm glad me and the girls chose well," said Elaine.

He three guys smiled, "well we have to go now and pick up our soon to be wives.

"Okay, see you at the courthouse, love you guys," said Elaine and Doug.

"Yea, you too, bye," said the three guys.

A few minutes later the girls Madison, Chelsea and Harper walked into the kitchen, "hey mom and dad, how do we look?" asked the girls.

"Oh wow, you girls look absolutely beautiful," said Elaine and Doug.

"Thanks mom and dad," said the girls. "Well, our soon to be husbands will be here any minute."

"Okay, love you girls," said Elaine and Doug.

"Yea love you too," said the girls. Suddenly a knock sounded at the door, "oh gosh they're here," and so Elaine, Doug and the girls headed into the family room. Doug walked over and opened the door and there stood Dante, Derek and Aaron, "hey guys."

"Hey Mr. Hollingsworth," said the guys, and so Doug immediately stepped out of the way, "wow you girls look absolutely beautiful."

"Thanks, and you guys look handsome too," said the girls.

"Well now, are you girls ready to go?" the guys asked.

"Yes, we are," said the girls. "Great, well let's go," said the guys.

CHAPTER 84

Three hours later the huge group of family and friends were heading back to Elaine and Doug's house for the wedding reception.

CHAPTER 85

Thirty minutes later the Hollingsworth's house was filled with wall to wall people celebrating the marriages of Trevor, Jana, Trenton, Deanne, Gabe, Erin, Chelsea, Derek, Madison, Aaron, Harper and Dante.

CHAPTER 86

Midnight rolled around, and all of the guests were all leaving out.

CHAPTER 87

After everyone had gone, Elaine and Doug turned to face their six newly married kids, "wow we're so proud of you, you six have grown up right before our eyes and we can't believe that you all are leaving so soon it doesn't seem possible," said Elaine and Doug.

"Yea, us either but don't worry were all going to keep our plans of graduating from high school, going through with our college and career plans, basically just starting our own lives, we promise we're not going to let marriage and babies get in the way of our dreams and careers and we promise that we'll make everything work," said the kids.

"Oh wow, that's great to hear kids that's what we've been praying, wanting and hoping for," said Elaine and Doug.

"Great, well it looks like you two got your prayers answered," said the kids.

"Yea, you're right, we did," said Elaine and Doug.

"Well mom and dad we hate to rush off, but we need to be going to our new homes, we're not far away from you two and yes mom and dad you'll be needed as helping grandparents," said the kids.

"Great, we're looking forward to it," said Elaine and Doug.

"Good," said the kids, and then immediately hugs were passed around, and then afterwards the kids were gone.

CHAPTER 88

After their second bunch had left to start their own lives, Doug and Elaine looked at one another, "oh wow."

"Oh my, gosh we've raised twelve wonderful strong kids and now they're all grown and gone starting their own lives," said Elaine.

"Yea, so now, what will we do?" Doug asked.

"I don't know but I have a few suggestions," said Elaine.

"Alright, like what?" Doug asked.
"Well, I say we go home and enjoy the peace and quiet of our home for now because soon we'll be overrun with

lots and lots of grandbabies to enjoy and to help with," said Elaine.

"Yea, you're right, and I can't wait," said Doug.

"Yea, I know, me either," said Elaine.

"Well come on let's go enjoy our empty home, peace and quiet."

"Yea let's," said Doug.

CHAPTER 89

While Doug was at work, Elaine was cleaning house and going through her kid's rooms boxing everything up and getting ready for whatever comes up next. Suddenly the phone started ringing, great I wonder who that can be, and she pulled out the home phone and answered it, "hello."

"Hey mom, it's Chelsea." "Oh, hey dear," said Elaine. "So, how's everything going dear?"

"Great," said Chelsea. "That's good to hear," said Elaine.

"So, mom, what're you doing right now?" asked Chelsea.

"Well dear, if you must know I'm cleaning house and boxing up all you kid's things," said Elaine.

"Oh okay," said Chelsea. "So dear, what can I do for you?" Elaine asked.

"Nothing really, I was just calling to check in and also to let you and dad knows that Derek and I are expecting twins," said Chelsea.

"Oh wow, how exciting, that's great," said Elaine.

"Yea, I know, we're so excited and we can't wait," Chelsea said.

"Yea, I bet," said Elaine. "Well congratulations dear."

"Thanks mom," said Chelsea. "Yea sure you're welcome," said Elaine.

"Mom, I'm worried about T.J., K.C. and D.J.," said Chelsea.

"Oh really, why dear?" asked Elaine.

"Well, it seems like all they do is work, they have no special lady in their lives," said Chelsea.

"Yea, well dear all I can say is don't worry about them, when the time is right, they'll meet their matches or soulmates," said Elaine.

"Oh, okay whatever you say," said Chelsea.

"Look dear, it's in God's hands and God runs on his time not ours," said Elaine.

"Yea, alright whatever," said Chelsea.

"Anyway, listen dear, you have enough to worry about than worrying about your older brothers they can take care of themselves," Elaine said.

"Yea, alright whatever you say mom," said Chelsea.

"Well mom I hate to rush off, but I have to get ready for graduation practice."

"Okay dear, have fun," said Elaine.

"Yea sure, bye mom," said Chelsea.

"Bye dear," said Elaine, and then she hung up and went back to what she was doing, when suddenly the phone started ringing again, oh jeez again, and so she quickly retrieved the phone and answered, "hello."

"Hey mom, it's Madison." "Oh, hey dear, how's everything going?" Elaine asked.

"Everything's fine I was just checking in and letting you and dad know that Aaron and I are expecting twins," said Madison.

"Oh wow, that's exciting, well congratulations dear," said Elaine.

"Thanks mom, we're really excited and can't wait," said Madison.

"Yea, I bet," said Elaine. "Mom I hate to bother you, but I'm worried about our big brothers," said Madison.

"Oh yea, why?" asked Elaine. "Well, it seems like all they do is work nonstop, they have no special ladies in their lives at this time," said Madison.

"Yea alright, well dear I'm going

to tell you the same thing I told your sister Chelsea, listen carefully, your older brothers can take care of themselves you have nothing to worry about your older brothers, when the times right they'll meet their soulmates it's in God's hands and He runs on his time not ours," said Elaine.

"Okay sure, whatever you say mom," said Madison. "Well mom, hate to cut this short but I have to go get ready for graduation practice."

"Oh, okay well have fun dear," said Elaine.

"Yea sure, bye mom," said Madison.

"Bye dear," said Elaine, and then she hung up, talking to herself okay let's try this again, and so she started back on her chore when the phone started ringing again, alright maybe not, and so she retrieved the phone answering, "hello."

"Hey mom, it's Harper." "Oh, hey dear," said Elaine. "So, how's everything going?"

"Everything's going good," said Madison. "What about you mom?"

"Everything's fine but busy," said Elaine.

"Great." "Well mom, I was just calling to check in and letting you know that Dante and I are expecting twins," said Harper.

"Oh wow, that's exciting news, congratulations dear," Elaine said.

"Thanks mom," said Harper. "Yea sure, you're welcome," said Elaine.

"Mom, I hate to bother you, but I'm worried about our older brothers," said Harper.

"Oh yea, why though?" Elaine asked.

"Well, it seems like all they do is work nonstop," said Harper.

"Yea, I know, look I'm going to tell you like I told your sisters Chelsea and Madison, so listen, Harper dear you have too much on your plate to even worry about your older brothers, and besides they can take care of themselves, when it's the right time your brothers will find their soulmates it's in Gods hands not ours, He runs on His time not ours," said Elaine.

"Okay whatever you say mom," said Harper. "Well mom, I hate to cut this short I have to go get ready for graduation practice," said Harper.

"Oh, sure honey, have fun," said

Elaine.

"Yea sure, bye mom," said Harper.

"Bye dear," said Elaine, and then Elaine hung up for the third time, and instead of picking up where she left off cleaning, she instead decided to call Doug, and so Elaine quickly dialed Doug's direct line.

A minute or two later his voice came on the line, "hello this is Detective Hollingsworth speaking."

"Hey honey," Elaine said. "Oh, hey babe, what's up?" Doug asked.

"Nothing much, I was just calling to let you know that I just received calls from our three youngest daughters," said Elaine.

"Oh yea, so what did they have to say?" Doug asked.

"Well first it looks like we're expecting six new grandbabies," said Elaine.

"Oh jeez," said Doug. "Yea honey, it's starting," said Elaine.

"Yea, I know," said Doug. "Honey, all three girls seemed to be worried about their three older brothers," said Elaine.

"Oh yea, why?" asked Doug. "Well honey the girls are saying their older brothers are work alcoholics, in which they work nonstop, which they don't have ladies in their lives," said Elaine.

"Oh, okay that's all," Doug said. "Yea," said Elaine.

"Well babe, did you tell them not to worry about their big brothers, that they're perfectly capable of taking care of themselves, it's all in God's hands not ours," Doug said.

"Yes honey, I told them all of this and then some," said Elaine.

"Alright then, don't worry about it anymore," said Doug.

"Okay whatever," said Elaine. "Well babe, I'm being paged I've got to go for now, we'll talk later," Doug said.

"Okay bye," said Elaine, and then she heard click, but immediately the phone started ringing again, and so she answered, "hello."

"Hey mom, it's Gabe." "Oh, hey son," said Elaine. "How's everything going?"

"Everything's going good," said Gabe. "Mom the reason I'm calling is to just check in and to let you know

Erin and I are expecting twins," said Gabe.

"Oh wow, that's exciting news, congratulations," said Elaine.

"Thanks mom," said Gabe. "Mom, by the way I'm letting you know now that I'm not worried about T.J., K.C. and D.J., they're old enough to take care of themselves and besides I for one don't think they're ready to settle down right now but who knows I could be wrong."

"Yea, I agree son, you're right about your outlook on your older brother's lives," said Elaine.

"Thanks mom," said Gabe. "Yea sure son, you're welcome," said Elaine.

"Well mom, I need to go for now," said Gabe.

"Okay son, love you," said Elaine. "Yea, I love you too mom, talk to you later," said Gabe, and then she herd click, but immediately the phone son started ringing again, oh jeez here we go again, and so she answered, "hello."

"Hey mom, it's Trenton." "Oh, hey son," said Elaine. "How's everything going?"

"Everything's going good," said Trenton.

"That's good to hear son," said Elaine.

"Hey mom the reason that I'm calling is to let you know that Deanne and I are expecting twins," said Trenton.

"Oh wow, that's awesome news, congratulations son," said Elaine.

"Thanks mom," said Trenton. "By the way I talked to our three sisters a little while ago and I think they should leave our older brothers alone they're grown, they can take care of themselves, so what if they work all the time that's them, and their prerogative they're not hurting anyone or anything."

"Yea, I know son and I agree with you," said Elaine.

"Okay great," said Trenton. "Well mom it's been great talking to you, but I really need to go for now."

"Sure alright, talk to you later son, love you," said Elaine.

"Yea love you too mom, bye," said Trenton.

"Yea bye son," said Elaine, and then she hung up and just sat there thinking about her conversations with her sons and daughters, while waiting for her last son to call because she knew he would and sure enough the phone started ringing again breaking her thoughts, and so she answered, "hello."

"Hey mom, it's Trevor." "Oh, hey son," said Elaine. "How's everything going?"

"Everything's going great," said Trevor.

"Well, that's good to hear," said Elaine.

"Listen mom, the girls called me saying they're worried about T.J., K.C. and D.C," said Trevor.

"Yea, I know and I kinda figured as much they called me and also your other two brothers," said Elaine.

"Oh yea," said Trevor. "Yea," said Elaine.

"Mom they need not to worry about them they're grown, they can take care of themselves, whatever's going to happen is going to happen." "Everything's in God's hands not ours He runs on His own time not ours," said Trevor.

"Yes son, I know this, and I've already told them this and more," said Elaine.   "Okay great," said Trevor. "Oh yea, before I forget Jana and I are expecting twins."

"Oh wow, that's great news, congratulations son," said Elaine.

"Thanks mom," said Trevor. "Yea sure, you're welcome," said Elaine.

"Well mom, I hate to cut this short I need to be going for now," said

Trevor.

"Oh, sure son, talk to you later," Elaine said.

"Yea okay, love you mom bye," said Trevor.

"Yea love you too son, bye," said Elaine, and then she hung up and then dialed Doug's direct line.   Within minutes his voice came through the line, "hello this is Detective Hollingsworth speaking."

"Hey honey," said Elaine. "Oh, hey babe, what's up?" Doug said.

"Nothing much, I just talked to the boys," said Elaine.

"Oh yea," said Doug. "Yea, and it seems that we're having six more twins," said Elaine.

"Oh wow," said Doug. "Yea, oh wow is right, and so that means the end of May we're going to have twelve new additions on top of the nine we already have," said Elaine.

"Yea it looks that way, wow we're going to be busy," said Doug.

"Yea busy being grandparents," said Elaine. "Honey the girls called they're worried about their older brothers."

"Oh yea, why?" asked Doug. "Well honey, it seems that the older boys have been working a lot, that they don't have time for personal relationships," said Elaine.

"Yea honey we've already talked about this and I'm telling you now that there is nothing to worry about, things will happen when they happen," Doug said. "Listen you and the girls can't just say poof and the boys have personal lives, it just doesn't work like that."

"Okay sure, I understand," said Elaine.

"Good now drop it, leave it alone all of you." "It's none of your business or the girls or anyone else's for that matter," said Doug.

"Yea okay, and thanks honey for the support," said Elaine.

"Yea sure, anytime," said Doug. "Well honey, I need to go for a while."

"Oh okay, sure," said Elaine.

CHAPTER 90

May twenty sixth, Wednesday morning rolled around, Elaine was busy in the kitchen cooking her six high school graduates a celebration dinner, when suddenly the phone started ringing, oh jeez I wonder, who that could be, and so she hurried over to the phone, and picked it up answering, "hello."

"Hey mom, it's Chelsea." "Oh, hey dear, what's up?" said Elaine.

"Nothing much, I was just wanted to call and check in and see what you're doing today," said Chelsea.

"Nothing really just working on a surprise for you graduates," said Elaine.

"Oh okay, well mom I was wondering, would you like to go baby shopping with me?" Chelsea said.

"Sure, why?" asked Elaine. "Well to be honest I want to be ready and prepared," said Chelsea.

"Okay that's understandable,"

said Elaine.

"Yea, I feel like I might have these babies anytime, so I feel the need to be prepared for the unthinkable," said Chelsea.

"Sure, but just remember that you have a big evening tomorrow," said Elaine.

"Yea, I know," said Chelsea. "Good," said Elaine. "So, when do you want to go?"

"Like today, in a couple of hours," said Chelsea.

"Oh, okay sure, I would love to go," said Elaine.

"Good, I'll pick you up at noon," said Chelsea.

"Okay great, see you then dear, bye," said Elaine.

"Okay bye mom," said Chelsea,

and then she hung up, and immediately it started ringing again, great gain, and so she answered, "hello."

"Hey mom, it's Madison." "Oh, hey dear, what's up?" asked Elaine.

"Nothing much, I was just wondering, what're you doing today?" asked Madison.

"Well, I'm trying to finish up a surprise for my graduates, but it looks like I'm going shopping with Chelsea," said Elaine.

"Oh okay," said Madison. "Why?" asked Elaine.

"Well, I was calling to see if you wanted to go shopping with me today for baby items?" Madison asked.

"Oh sure, what time?" asked Elaine.

"Noontime," said Madison. "Okay, well honey that's when I'm going with Chelsea," said Elaine.

"Oh okay, well why don't we go together?" asked Madison.

"Alright sure, let Chelsea know," said Elaine.

"Sure, I will," said Madison. "Okay great, see you at noon dear," Elaine said, and then she hung.

No sooner had Elaine clicked off the phone it immediately started ringing again, oh wow here we go again, and so she picked up the phone answering, "hello."

"Hey mom, it's Harper." "Oh, hey dear, what's up?" asked Elaine.

"Nothing much, mom I'm wondering, what're you doing today?" asked Harper.

"Well let's see I'm trying to finish up a surprise for my six graduates and I'm going shopping at noon with Chelsea and Madison for baby items, they seem to feel like their babies will be coming soon," said Elaine.

"Yea, well mom I feel the same way that's why I'm calling to see you wanted to go shopping with me today?" Harper said.

"Sure, we're leaving around noon, so you need to be here around noon or before," Elaine said.

"Okay sure, thanks mom," said Harper.

"Anyway, it doesn't hurt to be prepared."

"Yea, I know," said Elaine. "Well dear I'll see you soon."

"Yea alright mom," said Harper,

and then she hung up.

"Elaine quickly dialed Doug's direct line.

A couple of minutes later his voice came through the line, "hello this is Detective Hollingsworth speaking."

"Hey honey," said Elaine. "Oh, hey babe, what's up?" asked Doug.

"Nothing much," said Elaine. "Well, how's the cooking going?" asked Doug.

"It's not," said Elaine. "Oh yea, why?" asked Doug.

"Well let's see every time I tried to get started the phone rang and each time it was one of the girls," Elaine said.

"Oh yea, so what did they want?" Doug asked.

"Well, they want me to go baby shopping with them," said Elaine.

"Oh yea, why exactly?" Doug asked.

"Well honey they all feel like their babies are going to be here soon," said Elaine.

"Oh yea." "Wow." "Anyway, great and have fun," said Doug.

"Oh yea, loads, thanks," said Elaine.

CHAPTER 91

Before Elaine knew it twelve o'clock was upon her and soon after three cars pulled up in her driveway.

As she was walking out the door, her three daughters were walking towards her, "hey girls." "Hey mom," they said.

Hugs were quickly exchanged and soon after, "well, are you ready to go baby shopping for the day?" her girls asked.

"Yea just let me get the van out of the garage," Elaine said.

CHAPTER 92

Before they knew it, it was six o'clock and the group decided to call it a night.

"Jeez mom there's so much stuff here that we're not even sure if all of it will fit in our cars," said Chelsea, Madison and Harper.

"Yea, I know but we'll make it fit," said Elaine.

"Okay sure, thanks mom for

everything," said Chelsea, Madison and Harper.

"Yea sure, you're welcome," said Elaine.

"Well now let's get you girls heading home now you all have a very exciting and special day tomorrow."

"Yea, we do, we finally graduate from high school tomorrow and then soon after these babies will be here," said Chelsea, Madison and Harper.

"Yes, and that'll be a much-needed relief," Elaine said.

"Yea, you're not telling us anything we don't know already," the girls said.

"Yea, I guess so," said Elaine.

CHAPTER 93

Thirty minutes later Elaine pulled into her garage.

Minutes later the garage door opened up, and there was Doug, "hey babe and girls," he said.

"Hey honey," Elaine said. "Well let me help you ladies with all this stuff," said Doug.

"Sure, that would be great," Elaine said.

"Honey each of the bags are labeled with the girls names on them, so please load their cars with correct bags."

"Yes dear, I've got this under control," Doug said.

"Uh huh, alrighty then," said Elaine.

"Good," said Doug.

CHAPTER 94

Thirty minutes later Chelsea, Harper and Madison were on their way home to their husbands and new homes.

"Jeez honey you had a very busy day," said Doug.

"Yea you can say that again, and it's only going to get busier," said Elaine.

"Okay, why though?" asked Doug. "Well honey all three girls are experiencing the first signs of twinges," Elaine said.

"Oh jeez," said Doug. "That's great." "Yea they could go anytime," Elaine said.

"Oh jeez," said Doug. "Yea jeez," said Elaine.

"Anyway, so how was your shopping trip with the girls?" Doug asked.

"Great." "I believe we found everything that they ever wanted or needed," said Elaine.

"Good," said Doug. Now, how about we go and relax for the rest of the evening?"

"Yes, that sounds wonderful," said Elaine.

"Great," said Doug.

CHAPTER 95

May twenty seventh, Thursday morning rolled around, Elaine is in the kitchen working on the finishing of her special celebration dinner while Doug went into the office for a couple of hours, and all six kids are up at the school taking senior portraits and going over their valedictorian speeches.

CHAPTER 96

Elaine was in the kitchen, when suddenly the phone started ringing, and so she hurried and picked up the phone answering, "hello this is the Hollingsworth residence."

"Yes ma'am, I'm Mrs. Cathy Eastland, Derek's mom," she said.

"Oh, hi ma'am, so what can I do for you?" asked Elaine,

"Well let me say this first that I'm the spokesperson for the other parents," said Cathy. "Okay sure, so what can I do for you parents?" Elaine asked.

"Well ma'am we know the kids have to be at high school at five," said Cathy.

"Well, we parents were wondering, would it be alright with you if we came over around two o'clock all the moms to be exact?" asked Cathy.

"Wow sure that would be great," said Elaine.

"Great." "Well alright then we'll see you at two o'clock," said Elaine.

"Alright bye," said Cathy. "Yea bye," said Elaine, and then she hung up, and then Elaine quickly dialed Doug's direct line.

Within minutes his voice came through the line, "hello this is Detective Hollingsworth speaking."

"Hey honey," said Elaine. "Oh, hey babe, what's up?" asked Doug.

"Nothing much, but guess what?" Elaine said.

"I don't know, what?" asked Doug. "Well Derek's mom just called," said Elaine.

"Oh yea, what did she have to say?" Doug asked.

"Well, she and the other parents asked to do a small baby shower at our house at two o'clock, and honey I said yes," Elaine said.

"Great," said Doug. "Yea, so honey on your way home, will you pick up some finger foods, goodies and drinks?" said Elaine.

"Yea sure, I'm on my way now," Doug said.

"Great and thanks," said Elaine.

"Yea sure, no problems, see you soon," said Doug.

"Okay see you soon, bye," said Elaine.

CHAPTER 97

It was a little after twelve when Doug walked through the door loaded down with grocery bags heading to the kitchen.

A couple of minutes later he walked through the kitchen door, "hey babe."

She turned around, "oh hey honey, thank you honey, you're a lifesaver, you did a good job," said Elaine, as he was sitting the bags down.

"Thanks babe, and I'm glad I

could help," said Doug, as she started putting the items away until closer to time or the surprise baby-shower when suddenly their six kids walked through the door "hey mom and dad were here," said the kids.

"Hey kids, what a surprise," said Elaine and Doug.

"Yea well we wanted to stop by and see you both," the kids said.

"Oh okay, that's nice, so how was your picture day?" Elaine asked.

"It was fine, at least it's over with," said the kids.

"Alright good," said Elaine. "Anyway kids, we would like for you all to invite your husbands, wives and whoever else you want over for a awhile."

"Oh yea, why?" asked the kids.

"Well let's just say we have a surprise for you all starting at two o'clock," said Elaine.

"Oh wow, great, and yea we'll call them now," said the kids.

"Great," said Elaine.

CHAPTER 98

Forty-five minutes later the doorbell started buzzing, Doug quickly made his way over to the door and opened it up and there stood his new sons and daughters in laws, "new family, come on in," said Doug.

"Thanks," they said. "Sure," said the kids.

"Sure," said Doug, and then they started through the door.

As soon as they were inside the

hugs were passed around.

A minute or two later everyone stepped back, "Mr. Doug and Mrs. Elaine, thanks for having us," said the group.

"Of course, you're family, you're always welcome here," said Doug.

"Thanks," said the group. "So, mom and dad were anxious to know what this special surprise," said the group.

"Yea we know you'll find out soon enough but for now, how about you kids go hang out in the backyard until time," said Elaine and Doug.

"Okay whatever," said the kids.

CHAPTER 99

Twenty minutes later the doorbell

started buzzing, Elaine quickly headed over to the door and opened it up and there stood the parents of her newly sons and daughters in laws, "hi it's so nice to see you parents again," said Elaine.

"Yea, you too," said the parents. "Well welcome, come on in," said Elaine.

"Thanks," said the parents. "So, where do you want us?"

"The family room would be great," said Elaine.

"Great," said the parents, and then the group of parents headed towards the family room, while Elaine headed towards the kitchen.

As Elaine was making her way into the kitchen, when suddenly Chelsea came through the sliding glass doors, "who was that?"

"Well, if you must know that was your surprise," said Elaine.

"Really?" "Seriously?" "Are you kidding?" asked Chelsea.

"No, I'm not, now go on back to the group until I come for you kids," said Elaine. "Aright," said Chelsea.

When Chelsea had left, Elaine hurried to the family room to see if the surprise was ready yet.

Elaine walked into the family room and she was in awe the room was so beautiful, "wow you ladies did amazing job," said Elaine.

"Thanks," said the ladies. "Well, are we ready?" asked Elaine.

"Yes, we are," said the ladies. "Great because the kids are getting anxious," said Elaine.

"Yea, we bet, we can imagine," said the ladies.

"Well let me go get them, it's ten minutes to two," said Elaine. "Okay," said the ladies.

CHAPTER 100

Elaine walked to the sliding glass doors and opened them up, "alright kids it's time," said Elaine. "Great," said the kids.

A minute or two later the group were heading inside immediately noticing the decorated room, the parents and the loaded down present table, "oh my, gosh." "Oh wow, this is amazing," said the kids. "Wow, what a surprise, you're all here."

"Yea welcome to your baby

and graduation shower," the ladies said.   "Oh wow, this is so awesome, thank you so much, this is so sweet and thoughtful of you all," said the kids.

"Yea sure, you're welcome but we wanted to do this for you kids," said the ladies.

The kids smiled, "great." "Excuse us kids for a minute," said Elaine and Doug, and so Elaine and Doug walked out of the room.

A few minutes later they walked back into the family room pushing loaded down carts of assortment of food, deserts and drinks, "okay everyone let the party begin," said Elaine and Doug.

CHAPTER 101

Before they knew it four o'clock was upon them and it was time for the six graduates to get ready and leave.

CHAPTER 102

By four thirty all six kids were getting into their vehicles.

CHAPTER 103

Elaine and Doug arrived at Duncansville High School auditorium around six o'clock.

As they were walking in the door a greeter met them, "hi I'm Josh Dickerson."

"Hi we're the Hollingsworth's," said Doug.

"Oh okay, you folks are on the far

left hand corner, and about middle ways down," said Josh. "Okay thanks," said Doug. "Yes sir," said Josh.

As soon as they got to their seats, Elaine looked at Doug saying, "I'm going to go find our kids and see them for a few minutes."

"Okay sure," said Doug. "I'll be back in a few minutes," said Elaine, and then she started heading back the same way she came, when Elaine suddenly heard someone calling her name and she immediately turned around and there stood her son Gabe, "hey mom."

"Hey son," said Elaine. "Mom, what're you doing here so early?" asked Gabe.

"Well, your dad and I wanted to come early to get good sears and of course to see all of you," said Elaine.

"Well, that's awesome," said Gabe. "Well mom, we're back here."

"Alright son," Elaine said, and so she followed her son back and soon she spotted the rest of her clan.

After spending a few minutes with each one of her kids, she then headed back to her seat.

Minutes later she was back at her seat, "so how are our children?" asked Doug.

"Very nervous but ready to get this graduation ceremony over with," said Elaine.

"Yea, I bet," said Doug. "Honey, by the way, the girls are starting to feel some signs of the beginnings of twinges," said Elaine.

"Oh yea," said Doug. "Really?"

"Seriously?"

"Yea, and I just hope they hold out until after the graduation ceremony," said Elaine.

"Yea, me too," said Doug.

CHAPTER 104

Six forty-five rolled around, Principle Edward Evans has finally made it to the front of the podium, "good evening extinguished guests and staff, thank you for coming out this evening for this special occasion, the graduating senior class of two thousand and forty two," said Principle Edward Evans.

CHAPTER 105

Three hours later the graduation ceremony was over, and all the graduates and their families were getting ready to go celebrate.

Elaine and Doug were waiting at the auditorium doors for their graduates which were making their way over.

As their clan walked up, congratulations kids, we are so proud of you," said Elaine and Doug.

"Thanks mom and dad," said the kids. "Now, can we go now none of us girls are feeling good," said the girls.

"Sure," said Elaine and Doug. "So, what's wrong?"

"Well, our lower backs hurt, and we just plain feel bad," said the girls.

"Oh okay, well let's go then," said Doug.

"Alright thanks," said the girls," and then everyone headed to vehicles.

CHAPTER 106

Fifteen minutes later Doug and their kids pulled into the driveway at the same time.

Minutes later the group were walking into the house and immediately after entering the girls and boys went straight to their old rooms.

Elaine quickly went to check on her three girls.

Minutes later she found them each lying on their beds with their husbands right beside them, "mom, this isn't good, this hurts," said

Chelsea, Madison and Harper.

"Yea, I know and I'm sorry girls," said Elaine. "So, what do you want to do?"

"Well, we guess we need to go to the hospital," said Chelsea, Harper and Madison.

"Alright," said Elaine, and so she left the room.

Minutes later Derek, Chelsea, Aaron, Madison, Dante, Harper, Doug and Elaine were all heading to the Duncansville Hospital.

CHAPTER 107

Fifteen minutes later all four cars pulled up in front of the hospital sliding glass doors.

Within minutes the three young

husbands raced in to fetch nurses and orderlies.

Minutes later here came Dante, Derek and Aaron followed by three nurses and orderlies.

It didn't take long to get the girls settled in wheelchairs and then everyone rushed back inside, Doctor Anderson and Nurse Sheree walked up, "hey ladies, what seems to be the problem?"

"Well, we're all hurting in our lower backs extremely bad, we think we're in possible labor," said Chelsea.

"Uh huh, you could be, let's take a look, shall we?" said Doctor Anderson.

Minutes later Chelsea, Madison and Harper were all put in rooms, while Doctor Anderson walked up to Mr. and Mrs. Hollingsworth and their three son in laws, "yes sir."

"Hi folks, I just wanted to let you know that I have assistant doctors who are going to be working alongside me," said Doctor Anderson.

"Oh okay, great," said Elaine and Doug.

"Yea that means each girl will have a doctor and nurse of their own," said Doctor Anderson.

"Great, but why though?" asked Doug and Elaine.

"Well, I feel like it will better serve them," Doctor Anderson said.

"Okay thanks," said Doug and Elaine.

"Sure," said Doctor Anderson. "Well now let's see Madison will have me and Nurse Sheree, and Harper will have Doctor Kenneth Harrison and

Nurse Caroline, and Chelsea will have Doctor Carter Holloman and Nurse Allie."

"Wonderful," said Elaine and Doug. "Great," said Doctor Anderson.

"Well let's get started." "Alright guys you need to go be with your wives now."

"Yes sir," said Derek, Dante and Aaron.

CHAPTER 108

Thirty minutes later all three doctors came out of the rooms, "okay folks all three girls are indeed in labor and it looks like we're going to have babies here soon," said Doctor Anderson.

"Oh wow, that's great news," said

Elaine and Doug.

CHAPTER 109

Two hours later Doctor Anderson, Doctor Harrison and Doctor Hollowman were walking down the hallway towards the waiting area.

Minutes later, "hey folks." "Hey Doctors, so what's the verdict?" asked Elaine and Doug. "Well folks I believe congratulations is in order," said the doctors.

"Oh wow," said Elaine and Doug. "Yea everything went great with your three daughters," said the doctors.

"Oh good," said Elaine and Doug. "Anyway folks, the young husbands are on their way down now to tell you the surprising news," said the doctors.

"Great and thanks," said Elaine and Doug.

"Sure, you're welcome," said the Doctors.

As the doctors were walking away, here came their three sons in laws walking up, "Mr. Doug and Mrs. Elaine we have a huge surprise for you," they said.

"Oh yea, what?" asked Elaine and Doug.

"Well Chelsea and I have a boy and a girl," said Derek.

"Wow congratulations," said Elaine and Doug.

"Thanks," said Derek. "Chelsea will tell you what we named them."

"Oh, okay great," said Elaine and Doug.

"I'm next, and Madison and I have

two girls," said Aaron.

"Oh wow. Congratulations," said Elaine and Doug.

"Thanks," said Aaron. "Madison will tell you what we've named them."

"Okay wonderful," said Elaine and Doug.

"Alright my turn, well Harper and I have two boys," said Dante.   "Oh wow, congratulations," said Elaine and Doug.

"Thanks," said Dante. "Harper will tell you what we've named them."

"Okay great," said Elaine and Doug. "Mrs. Elaine and Mr. Doug mom's, and babies are doing great, we couldn't have asked for better."

"Wow, that's awesome," said Elaine and Doug.

"Yea," said Dante, Derek and

Aaron.

"Well come on back and meet your six new grandbabies."

"Yes, we would love too," said Elaine and Doug.

"Great," said Dante, Derek and Aaron.

CHAPTER 110

The first room that they came to belonged to Harper and Dante, and so they knocked, and immediately heard, "come in."

"Oh my, gosh honey I'm so excited," said Elaine.

"Yea, me too," said Doug, and they opened the door and walked in, "hey Harper and Dante."

"Hey mom and dad," said Harper.

"Well come meet your new grandbabies," and so they hurried over, "mom and dad, this is Thomas Carter on the right and this is Timothy Allen on the left."

"Oh my, gosh they're beautiful," said Elaine and Doug.

"Thanks mom and dad," said Harper and Dante.

"Yea sure, you're welcome," said Elaine and Doug.

CHAPTER 111

They spent the next fifteen minutes with Harper, Dante and their new babies.

"Well now we hate to rush off, but we need to go meet the rest of our new grandbabies," said Elaine and

Doug.

"Okay sure," said Harper and Dante, and then Elaine and Doug headed out the door and down the hall.

They came up to the second door belonging to Madison and Aaron, "oh my, gosh here we go again, this is so exciting," said Elaine.

"Yea, no doubt," said Doug, and so they knocked, "come in," and so they immediately entered, "hey kids."

"Hey mom and dad, come and meet your two new granddaughters," said Madison, and so they hurried over, "well now this is Anne Jane on the right and this one on the left is Amery Kadance," said Madison and Aaron.

"Oh wow, their beautiful,

congratulations," said Elaine and Doug.

"Thanks," said Madison and Aaron. "Yea sure, you're welcome," said Elaine and Doug.

CHAPTER 112

They spent the next fifteen or so minutes with Madison, Aaron and their new babies.

"Well now we hate to rush off, but we have another set of grandbabies to go meet," said Elaine and Doug.

"Oh sure," said Madison and Aaron, and then Elaine and Doug walked out the door hand in hand heading down the hall.

The third and final room that they

came to belonging to Chelsea and Derek, "oh my, gosh here we go again," said Elaine and Doug, and so they knocked, "come in," and immediately the door opened up, and in walked Doug and Elaine, "hey kids."

"Hey mom and dad, come meet your two new additions," said Chelsea and Derek.

"Sure," Elaine and Doug, and so they hurried over, "we named our daughter Kara Anne, and we named our son Kyle Dawson," said Chelsea and Derek.

"Oh wow, their beautiful, congratulations," said Elaine and Doug.

"Thanks," said Chelsea and Derek. "Yea sure, you're welcome," said Elaine and Doug.

CHAPTER 113

They spent the next fifteen or so minutes with Chelsea, Derek and their new grandbabies.

CHAPTER 114

As Elaine and Doug were walking out the hospital doors, she turned to him, "oh wow." "Oh my, gosh we have six new grandbabies, and the best part is we get to enjoy them without raising them," said Elaine.

"Yea, I know," said Doug. "Now don't get me wrong I love and have enjoyed raising kids but it's time that our kids learn how to be responsible, and dependant on themselves."

"Yes honey, but I hate to say this,

but I think by tomorrow morning we're going to have more surprises," said Elaine.

"Yea could be," said Doug. Elaine smiled, "Oh wow, I'm so happy, excited and I can't wait."

"Yea me either," said Doug. "Now let's go home and rest up before more surprises come up."

"Yea sure," said Elaine.

CHAPTER 115

"It's four in the morning, and Elaine and Doug are snoozing away soundly, when suddenly the phone started ringing.

After four rings Elaine finally woke up enough to answer it, "hello."

"Hey mom, it's Gabe." "Oh, hey

son, what's wrong?" said Elaine.

"Erin is in labor and we're on our way to Duncansville Hospital," said Gabe.

"Oh okay, we're on our way," said Elaine and Doug.

"Great see you soon," said Gabe. "Yes son, see you soon," Elaine said, and then she hung up. "Doug honey."

"Yea, I'm up," said Doug. "Who was that at this ungodly hour?"

"Gabe just called to tell us that Erin is in labor and on their way to the Duncansville Hospital," said Elaine.

"Oh wow, well come on let's get up and get ready," said Doug.

"Yes sure," said Elaine.

CHAPTER 116

Fifteen minutes later they were walking out the door, when suddenly Elaine's phone started ringing again, and so she answered, "hello."

"Hey mom, it's Trenton." "Oh, hey son, what's up?" asked Elaine.

"Well, I'm calling to let you know that Deanne is in labor and we're enroot to the hospital now," said Trenton.

"Oh wow." "Okay this is crazy," said Elaine.

"Why mom?" asked Trenton. "Well Gabe just called and said that they are on their way to the hospital too," said Elaine.

"Oh wow, that's great," said Trenton. "Well mom it looks like you're going to have your other set of grandbabies."

"Yea it looks that way," said Elaine.

"Okay, well son we'll see you there."

"Yea see you there," said Trenton, and then she hung up.

"Wow again," said Doug. "Who was that?"

"Trenton," said Elaine. "Oh yea," said Doug.

"Yea it seems that he's taking Deanne to the Hospital," Elaine.

"Oh wow, that's great," said Doug.

"Yea, I agree," said Elaine. Just then her phone started ringing again, and so she answered, "hello."

"Hey mom, it's Trevor." "Oh, hey son, what's up?" asked Elaine.

"Well, I'm just calling to let you

know that we're on our way to the hospital Jana's in labor," said Trevor.

"Oh wow, that's awesome, we'll be there in a few minutes," said Elaine.

"Oh yea, why?" asked Trevor. "Well son it seems that your other two brothers are going through the same thing," said Elaine.

"Oh, okay great," said Trevor. "Wow this is cool." "Well see you in a few."

"Okay by son," said Elaine, and then she hung up.

"Who was that?" asked Doug. "Trevor letting us know that Deanne is in labor and they're on their way to the hospital," said Elaine. "Wow honey, I can't believe it all three girls are in labor right now."

"Wow honey we're in for a rude awakening."

"Yea, I know but I'm ready for it," said Doug.

"Yea, me too," said Elaine.
"Great," said Doug.

Minutes later four cars pulled up into the hospital circle drive, and soon after Doug and the three husbands went rushing inside to get nurses and orderlies, while Elaine stayed with young ladies comforting them.

A few minutes later Doug and the three husbands came back with three nurses and orderlies following closely behind.

CHAPTER 117

As soon as the girls wee settled

into their wheelchairs then the group rushed back inside, they noticed there were doctors already waiting for them, "good morning folks."

"Good morning," said Elaine and Doug.

"Hi folks, I'm Doctor Harrison, and this is Nurse Doreen, this is Doctor Anderson, and this is Nurse Helen, this is Doctor Hoffman and Nurse Kate."

"Now folks and girls, each one of you will be assigned a doctor and nurse team," said Doctor Harrison.

"Okay great," said the girls. "Now Erin you will be under the care of me Doctor Harrison and Nurse Helen," said Doctor Harrison.

"Okay great," said Erin. "Now Jana you will be under the care of Doctor Anderson and Nurse Doreen," said Doctor Harrison.

"Okay great," said Jana. "Now Deanne you will be under the care of Doctor Hoffman and Nurse Kate," said Doctor Harrison. "Alright let's get started, nurses let's get these girls settled in their rooms."

CHAPTER 118

Three hours later here came walking down the hallway the three nurses who are taking care of the girls their husband.

The three nurses came out to the waiting room, "hey Mrs. and Mr. Hollingsworth.

"Yes," said Elaine and Doug. "Folks we came to tell you that all three girls did wonderful, mom's and babies are doing wonderful," said the doctors.

"Thanks," said Elaine and Doug. "Yea sure, you're welcome," said the doctors. "The husbands will be out here in a few minutes."

"Okay great and thanks," said Elaine and Doug, and then the three nurses headed back down the hallway.

"Oh wow." "Oh my, gosh we have six more additions," said Doug.

"Yea, I know and I'm so excited, happy and relieved," said Elaine.

"Yea, me too," said Doug.

CHAPTER 119

Gabe, Trenton and Trevor started down the hall, "oh good, here they come," said Elaine.

Minutes later, "hey mom and dad." "Hey guys," said Elaine and Doug.

"Mom and dad we have some very exciting news for you both," the three guys said.

"Oh yea," said Elaine and Doug. "Yes ma'am, and sir," said the guys.

"Great, well let's hear it," said Elaine and Doug.

"Alright here it goes mom and dad, Erin and I have a girl and a boy," said Gabe.

"Oh son, that's great congratulations," said Elaine and Doug.

"Thanks," said Gabe. "Erin will tell you what we've named them."

"Oh, okay great," said Elaine and

Doug.

"I'm next mom and dad, Deanne and I have two boys," said Trenton.

"Oh wow, that's wonderful news, congratulations," said Elaine and Doug.

"Thanks," said Trenton. "Deanne will tell you what we've named them."

"Okay great," said Elaine and Doug.

"Alright my turn, mom and dad, Jana and I have two girls," said Trevor.

"Oh wow, that's terrific news, congratulations," said Elaine and Doug.

"Thanks," said Trevor. "Jana will tell you what we've named them."

"Okay great," said Elaine and Doug.

"Well come on back and meet

your six new additions," said the guys.

"Sure, we would love too," said Elaine and Doug.

"Great," said the guys, and so the group headed down the hall.

CHAPTER 120

The first room that they came to belonging to Erin and Gabe, "oh honey, I'm so excited and happy," said Elaine.

"Yea, me too," said Doug. "Now knock already."

"Yes dear," Elaine said, and so she knocked, and they immediately heard, "come in," and so they opened the door and they walked inside, "hey son and Erin."

"Hey mom and dad, come meet

your grand daughter and grandson," said Gabe.

"Sure," said Elaine and Doug, and so they hurried over, "well now this is your granddaughter McKenna Reece, and this is your grandson Micah Cain," said Erin.

"Oh wow, they're just beautiful, congratulations," said Elaine and Doug.

"Thanks," said Erin and Gabe.

CHAPTER 121

They spent the next fifteen or so minutes visiting with Gabe, Erin and their new grandbabies.

"Well, we hate to rush off, but we have four more grandbabies to go meet," said Elaine and Doug.

"Oh sure, see you soon," said Erin and Gabe.

As they were walking out the door, Elaine turned to Doug saying, "oh my, gosh I can't believe it we have six new grandbabies," said Elaine.

"Yea, I know," said Doug. "Honey we been very blessed," Elaine said.

"Yes, we have, no doubt," said Doug. "Well come on dear let's go see the next set."

"Yea, I'm ready," said Elaine.

CHAPTER 122

They walked up to the second door belonging to Deanne and Trenton, and so they quickly knocked, and immediately heard, "come in," and so they opened the door and walked inside, "hey Deanne and Trenton."

"Hey mom and dad, come meet your new grandsons," said Trenton.

"Sure," said Elaine and Doug, and so they hurried over, "this is Dawson Michael on the left and this is David Allen on the right," said Deanne.

"Oh wow, they're so beautiful, congratulations," said Elaine and Doug.

"Thanks," said Deanne and Trenton.

CHAPTER 123

They spent the next fifteen or so minutes visiting with Deanne, Trenton and their new grandbabies.

"Well, we hate to rush off, but we

have two more new   grandchildren to meet," said Elaine and Doug.

"Oh sure, see you soon," said Trenton and Deanne.

"Yes, we'll see you soon," said Elaine and Doug, and then they walked out the door heading down the hallway hand in hand.

A few minutes later they walked up to the third and final door belonging to Jana and Trevor, and they quickly knocked, and immediately they heard, "come in," and so they opened the door and walked inside, "hey Trevor and Jana.

"Hey mom and dad, come meet your two granddaughters," said Trevor and Jana.

"Sure," said Elaine and Doug, and so they hurried over, "this is Caitlyn

Jane on the right and this is Cassandra Kara on the left," said Jana.

"Oh wow, they're beautiful, congratulations," said Elaine and Doug.

"Thanks," said Jana and Trevor. "Yea sure, you're welcome," said Elaine and Doug.

CHAPTER 124

They spent the next fifteen or so minutes visiting with Jana, Trevor and their new grandbabies.

CHAPTER 125

A couple of hours later Elaine and Doug were on their way home, "wow honey I can't believe it we have six more new additions," said Elaine.

"Yea, I know and it's great," said Doug.

"Yea and just think we get to actually enjoy being grandparents," said Elaine.

"Yes, we do, and I'm so glad," said Doug.

"Good," said Elaine. "Well now, what do you say let's go home and relax and enjoy peace and quiet for right now?" Doug said.

"Yes, that sounds great," said Elaine.

"Good," said Doug.

CHAPTER 126

A week later on June tenth Trenton, Trevor, Gabe, Madison,

Harper and Chelsea and their families came home from the hospital and everyone is doing wonderful.